STARSHIP BLOOPERS

STARSHIP BLOOPERS

BY THE AUTHOR OF *THE ZOMBIE CHASERS*
JOHN KLOEPFER

ILLUSTRATED BY
NICK EDWARDS

HARPER
An Imprint of HarperCollinsPublishers

Library of Congress Control Number: 2015943567
ISBN 978-0-06-223106-2

Typography by Ray Shappell
16 17 18 19 20   CG/RRDH   10 9 8 7 6 5 4 3 2 1
❖
First Edition

For Mary, Jim, Barbara, Dennis, Linda, Charlie,
Little Mary, Devon, Chad, Connor, Tim, and Matt

The smell of scorched flesh and alien slime drifted through the night air.

The entire science camp reeked like a bonfire that had just been peed on.

Only a few minutes ago Kevin Brewer and his friends—Warner Reed, Tara Swift, TJ Boyd, and an alien cyborg cop named Klyk—had almost been blown up by two of the most dangerous aliens in the galaxy. Zouric and Nuzz were trying to turn the human race into a bunch of robo-slaves. But luckily for the inhabitants of planet Earth, the four friends had used their wormhole generator to blast the evil aliens across the galaxy.

Kevin glanced through the crowd of campers, who were all a bit shell-shocked from the extraterrestrial invasion. Alexander stared back at him with a dirty-diaper scowl on his face. Kevin broke off eye contact with his nemesis and looked over at their head counselor, Mr. Dimpus. The camp director and the other counselors were gathered in a circle, whispering to one another.

For the past eight hours or so, a freeze-ray bomb had immobilized the camp and everyone in it except for Kevin and his friends. The girls' soccer campers from across the lake, as well as an alien race of reptilian warriors, known as Kamilions, had been brainwashed by alien nanobugs designed by Zouric and Nuzz.

It was a lot to process, and Kevin could tell that nobody really knew what was going on. *Probably better that way*, he thought. Kevin wished they had a memory eraser like in the movies, but he'd just have to hope that it would all blow over somehow.

The odds of that happening, he knew, were slim.

In the past twenty-four hours Kevin and his friends had gone from science-camp dorks to interstellar crime fighters who had saved the world not once, but twice in a single day. First thing that morning, before taking down Zouric and Nuzz, they had stopped Mim, a furry purple alien with a mean appetite, from eating their planet.

Kevin couldn't take all the credit, though. If it weren't for a little help from Klyk, their intragalactic bounty hunter friend, the planet would now be brainwashed and their camp would still be frozen in time. They were short a wormhole generator and some forcefield gloves. But along with two freeze rays and a shrink ray, there was one other special thing that they had in their possession.

"Let me see that comic book again," Kevin said, and snapped his fingers at TJ.

TJ handed him Max Greyson's latest comic book. The newest edition of the famous comic book series *Brainstorm* had just come through an alien transmitter, materializing as if by magic. Even weirder than that, all the illustrations showed Kevin and his friends taking down Zouric and Nuzz, which had *just* happened. It was almost as if the famous comic book creator had seen the events before they happened.

But that wasn't all Max had sent. His transmission also said he was being held captive in outer space. The entire galaxy, he also said, was in grave danger. Kevin and his friends needed to rescue him before something really bad happened.

What that was, exactly, they had no idea.

They all peered over Kevin's shoulders as he flipped through the comic book. Tara shone a flashlight to see the pages in the dark. "You guys notice anything?"

"Not really, except us being awesome and saving the world!" Warner said.

"The page numbers," Tara gasped. "They're out of order!"

"Maybe that's because they're not page numbers," Kevin said.

"Exactly!" TJ started to write down the digits in a sequence: 2, 3, 5, 13, 89, 233, 1597.

"Do these look familiar?" He showed Kevin, Warner, Tara, and Klyk.

"Two, three, five, and thirteen are all prime

numbers," Kevin said, the wheels turning in his head.

"And eighty-nine, two hundred thirty-three, and fifteen ninety-seven," Tara said. "Those are all primes, too, but they're also part of the Fibonacci sequence. . . ."

Klyk leaned over them as they studied the comic. "Those are coordinates," Klyk told them. "Somewhere

in the Globula Nebula. Near the outer quadrant of the Centaurus arm of the Milky Way."

"Max is telling us where he is!" Warner exclaimed. "I knew he wouldn't leave us hanging like that."

"But that's, like, sixty thousand light years away!" TJ exclaimed. "On the other side of the galaxy."

"Then we better gear up," Warner said, looking through his bag of alien gadgets. "We have two freeze rays and one shrink ray."

"One transmitter," TJ said, and held up the device that had sent the comic book through space and time.

"We should get the telepathy helmet before we go, too," Tara said.

"Who cares about the telepathy helmet?" said Warner. "Let's go find Max Greyson."

"No, she's right," said Klyk. "Telepathy helmets are hard to come by, if not impossible. I have no idea how Mim got one in the first place."

Tara had left the telepathy helmet inside one of the girls' cabins at the soccer camp.

Kevin, Warner, Tara, TJ, and Klyk sprinted off into

the shadowy forest, leaving the rest of the campers and counselors behind. They wove through the trees until they hit the lake. Kevin led the way as they skirted the lake and made their way through the girls' soccer camp.

"Let's go," Klyk said, and pushed the cabin door open with his bionic arm. The kids ducked under and ran inside.

The floorboards creaked as they walked through the empty cabin. Zack's eyes swept back and forth across the floor. The telepathy helmet stuck out from beneath one of the beds.

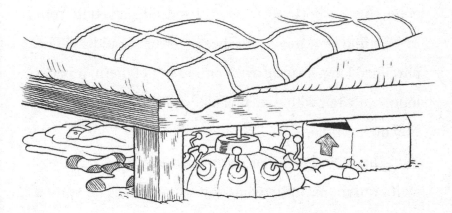

Kevin shuffled across the mattress and hopped off the other side. The high-tech headgear glinted in the moonlight. He bent down and was about to pick up the helmet when a cylinder of magenta light appeared in front of him. The thick beam of light was perfectly round and cast a reddish-purple glow throughout the room.

"What the—" Kevin jumped back, startled. He flinched at the sight in front of him.

An alien had appeared that looked like a giant hairless cat with four eyes across its brow. The feline-esque creature stood on two hind legs and was as big as a tall human, only a few inches shorter than Klyk. Kevin counted six arms total, three on each side, starting from its hips and working up its ribcage to the shoulders. The paws had long, sharp claws coming out of them. It had a long, scaly tail with dinosaur-like spikes that ran all the way up its spine.

The alien looked at them with all four of its eyes as its tail menacingly whapped to and fro. The spikes on its back prickled like a porcupine's as Klyk's hand went slowly for his hip, like a Wild West gunslinger getting ready for a duel.

"Hold it right there!" Klyk said calmly. "Don't move."

But the alien didn't listen. It quickly bent down and snatched up the telepathy helmet in its sixfold clutches.

Klyk drew a small gadget, aimed it at the alien, and fired. Kevin stepped back.

A bolt of electric-blue light zapped across the room and struck the alien in the arm. The beast squawked and disappeared into its magenta beam of light, along with the telepathy helmet held tightly in its paws.

"Did everybody see that?" Tara asked. "'Cause I want to make sure I'm not the only one who just saw a seven-foot, four-eyed cat with six arms and a dinosaur tail. . . ."

"What the heck was that thing?" Kevin asked.

All the kids gazed up at Klyk, who was putting the small remote-control-like gadget back in his hip holster. "That, my friends, was a Sfink. . . ."

"And what's that thing you just shot it with?" TJ asked.

"That was a tracking device," Klyk said. "Give it a minute and it should tell us where he went with our helmet."

"Cool," Warner said. "But what's a Sfink?"

"They're kind of like space pirates," he said. "They're very unfriendly. I've actually never seen one in person. But I've heard stories."

"What kind of space cop are you?" Warner shook his head.

"The galaxy's huge," Klyk said defensively. "I'm more familiar with the aliens in my sector. We've never had a problem with the Sfinks in my neck of the galaxy. Phirf and Drooq would know more about it."

"Who are Phirf and Drooq?" Kevin asked.

"My partners," he said. "The ones *you* zapped with the wormhole generator. They will know more about the Sfinks than I do, since they work in the outer sectors. That's where some of the more unsavory aliens spend their time."

"It doesn't make sense, though," Kevin said. "Why would this alien randomly want our telepathy helmet?"

"I don't think it was random," Tara said.

"But, how did it know that we even had a telepathy helmet?" Kevin said.

"It must have been watching us somehow," TJ suggested.

"Like, it knew exactly where we were," said Warner.

"That's okay, because now we know exactly where

it is . . . check it out." Klyk showed them the readout from the tracking device.

Kevin's eyes bulged with excitement.

The numbers on Klyk's tracker were precisely the same coordinates as the pages of Max Greyson's comic book.

The wheels turned in Kevin's mind. The Sfink was in the same place as the coordinates Max had given them. What did that mean? Did the Sfinks have Max? Were they the ones who were holding him captive? And if so, what were they after? And why were they interested in the telepathy helmet?

Kevin didn't have any of the answers yet. But he knew what they had to do. They had to go to outer space and figure out what was going on.

The five of them left the cabin and ran back through the woods. Klyk's spaceship was right where they'd left it on the outskirts of camp. Through the trees, Kevin could see the counselors trying to regain order.

"Let's get out of here before the counselors realize we're gone," Tara said.

"Too late." Kevin heard a rustle in the grass and whipped his head around.

"Not so fast," Dimpus said. Their head counselor ducked under a few low-hanging branches of a pine tree. "No one's going anywhere if I have anything to say about it."

TJ looked at Klyk and raised his eyebrows. "You wanna take care of this?"

Klyk walked up to Dimpus, towering over the camp counselor. "Let's have a talk. . . ."

Dimpus tilted his head back and stared up at the  giant alien cyborg, his voice trembling. "M-m-mister, I don't know who you are or where you came from, but I can't let y-y-you . . ." Dimpus's voice trailed off.

"I understand you are only looking out for the well-being of these children," Klyk said. "But they are now part of an intragalactic investigation. I can assure you I will look after them and I give you my word that no harm will come to them."

Kevin rolled his eyes. *At least Klyk's a good liar*, he thought.

Dimpus's brow crinkled and his eyes narrowed to a squint.

"I pinky swear." Klyk curled his littlest finger and held it out.

"Pinky swear," Dimpus said, and hooked his pinky with Klyk's little finger. "Don't let me down." Dimpus took two steps back and saluted his campers.

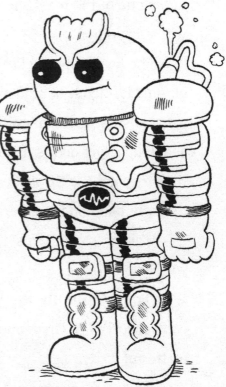

Kevin and his friends followed Klyk onto his spaceship.

"Good luck, my little scientists!" Dimpus called up from the ground.

 "How do you know about pinky swears?" Tara asked Klyk.

Klyk pointed at the side of his head that held his robotic brain. "I tapped into your network servers and downloaded some of your most highly valued customs onto my hard drive. According to your internet, pinky swearing is one of the most sacred bonds you humans make with each other."

The four humans climbed up into Klyk's ship. Klyk closed the hatch behind them, and they all took their usual positions. The alien sat down in the main captain's seat like a king on his throne. He cracked his knuckles, then gripped the throttle with his left hand and placed his right hand on the steering controls.

Warner cleared his throat. "What do you think you're doing?"

"I'm going to fly this ship into outer space so we can rescue Max Greyson from the Sfinks," Klyk said matter-of-factly.

"Huh?" Warner said. "No, no, I think you're

confused. I'm the captain. This is my ship!"

"You're a funny little human, aren't you?" Klyk said. "Now sit down and buckle up."

The spaceship rumbled to life and the interior lights dimmed. The control panels lit up with a neon glow and the flatscreens lining the control boards scrolled with data for takeoff. A low hum filled the cabin, and Kevin looked at Warner. A huge smile stretched across his friend's face, and his eyes were bugging out of his head. Warner pointed toward the sky and mouthed the words *this is really happening.*

Kevin could hardly believe it.

TJ was more thrilled than any of them. Their little friend bounced in his seat with a goofy look on his face, clapping his hands excitedly as they prepared to blast off.

"Don't we need spacesuits or something?" Tara asked.

"Not necessary," Klyk said. "The ship's gravitation is carefully calibrated and the cabin is climate controlled. All the planets we'll be going to are within Earth's range

of livability, so you'll all be safe."

Kevin's stomach dropped as they lifted up into the sky, as if he were in an elevator about to stop. It felt like a million little butterflies were fluttering around in his belly. Kevin could hardly believe it. They were actually going to outer space.

Like, for real.

Klyk tapped a couple holographic buttons that hung in midair on translucent touch screens.

"What's all that?" Tara asked, waving her hand at the computer.

"I'm just plotting our course through the wormhole superhighway. That's how we'll get to the coordinates."

Klyk then pushed the accelerator, and they shot

straight up into the stratosphere.

"Is there an antigravity drive on this thing?" TJ piped up. "There must be, right?"

"There is . . . unless, oh no! Are we about to get ripped apart from the g-force?" said Klyk.

TJ's eyes crinkled. "So there is one."

"Yeah, there is one," Klyk said. "But don't worry about it."

"What kind of propulsion system are we using?" TJ asked.

"The kind that gets us where we need to go," Klyk said. "Now stop asking so many questions, sit back, and relax."

The kids watched their home planet get tinier and tinier as they zipped past Mars, wove through the asteroid belt, and shot toward Jupiter.

The gaseous planet was bigger than Kevin had ever imagined. He knew in his head that Jupiter was 318 times more massive than Earth, but only now did it really sink in what that meant. It was the difference between knowing something and seeing it firsthand. They were two completely different things.

It suddenly dawned on Kevin just how enormous the galaxy and the universe really were. And how teeny they were in comparison.

"This is, like, the coolest thing that's ever happened to me," Tara said. "And I once met Taylor Swift."

"Wow, that's really saying something." Warner rolled his eyes. "Not."

Klyk put the ship into hyperdrive and they zoomed through outer space.

"Dude, check it out." Kevin's jaw dropped as he looked out the viewport. "It's Saturn!"

As they whizzed past the multi-ringed planet, Tara spun around in her seat. "Klyk, slow down a little!" she yelled. "Believe it or not, some of us have never been to space before."

"Sorry, kid, this isn't a sightseeing tour," Klyk said, and kept on accelerating faster and faster.

Kevin wished they could slow down, too, but he knew they had to keep going. The Sfinks had Max Greyson, and apparently the entire galaxy was in jeopardy. They knew the *what* and the *where*. Now they just had to figure out the *how* and the *why*.

Just then the fabric of time and space seemed to open up like a portal and they zipped full-throttle into a large swirling wormhole. It was like getting sucked down the whirlpool in a draining bathtub.

In a split second, the starscape of outer space disappeared and they were in a warp tunnel of space-time—red and green rays stretched with blue and white beams. Despite the swirling colors around him, Kevin couldn't even feel the shift in direction. *The antigravity drive must be working,* he thought.

"What is this thing?" Warner yelled at their alien ship captain while gripping his seat.

"Welcome to the wormhole superhighway," he told them. "Constructed a millennium ago by the IF, who were able to extend wormholes to certain portions of the galaxy for quick interstellar travel."

"What's the IF?" TJ asked.

"The Intragalactic Federation," Klyk told them. "They make the laws for all the different star systems in the Milky Way galaxy. If there are ever any threats to the galaxy, the IF is on the job."

"Well, shouldn't we be calling them then?"

"Sorry, Warner, but a missing Earthling and a stolen telepathy helmet don't exactly get the IF's attention. They work on real threats, not petty misdemeanors."

"But Max's message," Kevin said, waving their comic book at Klyk. "He said the whole galaxy was in grave danger."

"Fine," Klyk said. "We can call for backup once we get to our destination."

A few minutes later they came out of the spiraling time warp. As they shot out of the wormhole, Klyk yelped in surprise and jerked a hard left, then a sharp right to slow them down.

"Dude, what the heck?" Warner said, holding on to his seat to keep steady.

"There's an asteroid belt," Klyk said, steering and swerving like a madman. "It shouldn't be here!"

The large floating boulders sailed past Kevin's window, only a few feet away.

"Klyk, heads up!" TJ shouted. "There's a big one coming up on our left!"

The ship jerked to the right and they barely dodged the asteroid.

KABAM!

"What was that?" Tara yelled, as a smaller asteroid sideswiped them. The ship spun as the asteroid bounced off the side and Klyk struggled to keep them level.

"Hold on!" he shouted. Kevin could see a crisscrossing obstacle course of asteroids in front of him.

Kevin braced himself, preparing for impact. They were about to ram into a huge rock when all of a sudden, the laser cannon fired and blew the asteroid into a zillion pieces.

"Woo-hoo!" Warner yelped.

"Nice shot, buddy!" Kevin yelled to him.

"Don't celebrate too soon, boys," Klyk warned them. "We're not out of the woods just yet."

As they wove through the rocky debris, a new threat

 appeared.

Kevin's stomach dropped and a panicky dread washed over him.

They were drifting into the rear of a fleet of black battle cruisers, hovering in attack forma-tion. The black cruisers were facing off against a fleet of silver spaceships.

"Who are these guys? And where are we?" Tara asked, a bit of fear in her voice.

"It looks like we're above planet Glomm," Klyk said. "I recognize the Glomms' silver cruisers. But I don't know who they're fighting."

Kevin looked to see who was flying the black space-ships. Squinting through the windshield, Kevin saw a huge, hairless, misshapen cat with four eyes above its wet, slimy nose. It had humongous ears springing off the sides of its head with little squiggly ten-tacles coming out of them.

It was the same four-eyed alien beast they had seen back in the cabin, the one who stole their telepathy helmet.

"It's the Sfinks!" Kevin said.

Then the black battleships pivoted in their formation, aiming directly at their ship.

Klyk flipped the invisibility shield on and tried to slip away. One of the enemy cruisers charged up with a neon-red glow. Two large laser cannons dropped beneath the hull.

"I thought they couldn't see us," Tara said.

"They must have invisibility scanners on their ships," Klyk said.

"Well, what's the point of invisibility shields if everybody has invisibility scanners?" Tara shouted.

"Not everyone has invisibility scanners, smarty-pants," the alien's voice boomed. "They're hard to come by!"

"Everybody, chill out!" TJ called for a truce. "We gotta get out of here!"

The laser cannons powered up on the enemy space cruiser, ready to fire, and Klyk slammed the accelerator. Their spaceship lurched forward as the Sfinks' laser cannons exploded in two wide streaks of light.

Klyk's spaceship zipped between the alien forces just as the standoff erupted in a flurry of flashes. The vast, starry black of outer space lit up like a lightning storm from all the laser beams.

Klyk's ship wove through the crossfire and photon blasts. Kevin bumped around in his seat. His head knocked on the high metal sides of the gunner's chair.

Both of the alien fleets split into smaller formations and clashed in an aerial dogfight, hundreds of ships whirling around in complex spirals.

"Everybody!" Klyk shouted over the shrieking of photon blasts. "Man the cannons! Fire at will!"

Their spacecraft dipped steeply and they dropped below the crossfire.

"Klyk, get us out of here!" Kevin hollered.

"That's what I'm trying to do!"

"Do or do not," Warner said. "There is no *try*!"

"Look out!" Tara shrieked, and dove out of her seat and onto the floor.

A huge explosion hit the outside of the ship. Tara's laser cannon backfired, destroying the control panel in a puff of thick smoke.

The aftershock rippled through the cockpit. Klyk

rocked from side to side, losing control of the steering.

"Hang on!" Klyk yelled.

Klyk smacked a button on the side of his seat, and the turbo thrusters propelled them forward with a quick jolt. The spaceship broke through the outer atmosphere of Glomm and headed toward the planet's surface.

The ship spun out and Kevin felt like he was on the cup ride at a carnival. He was afraid he might get sick. His stomach started to churn and he tried to focus on the planet rotating beneath them. He steadied his gaze and tried to stay calm.

Planet Glomm had a circular region that was lush and green. The forested land was surrounded by stark, endless badlands, like an oasis in the middle of a desert. Around the desert, there was a vast ocean. The planet looked something like Earth might have a billion years ago, before Pangaea split up into the continents.

"Klyk, we're gonna be all right, right?" TJ called as they plunged toward the ground, gripping the armrests of his seat like a terrified kid in a dentist's chair.

Klyk ignored him and focused on the task at hand.

"I'm serious, man, I don't want to die!"

"Be quiet, TJ!" Tara shouted, equally frightened. "And let the alien do his thing!"

"Not trying to say I'm the best or anything," Warner called out. "But if I'd been flying, we never woulda got hit."

"Get ready!" Klyk called out from the front. "Hang on tight. . . ."

Kevin winced and tensed up as they crash-landed with a *plunk*.

They skidded to a stop, and Kevin reopened his eyes. He was curled up in a ball, strapped into his seat. He peered out of the viewport of the spaceship, checking out the alien terrain.

Something was churning out of the dirt, emerging out of the ground, like a giant insect. It was some subterranean vehicle with a spinning drill bit on its nose. The machine surfaced and drove right next to their crashed spaceship.

Warner stood next to Kevin and looked through the viewport.

Eight aliens stepped out of the burrowing vehicle and hopped to the ground, surrounding Klyk's ship.

Kevin unbuckled himself from the seat. "Klyk, get us out of here. We've got company. . . ."

"We're not going anywhere," Klyk said. "The engine is shot!"

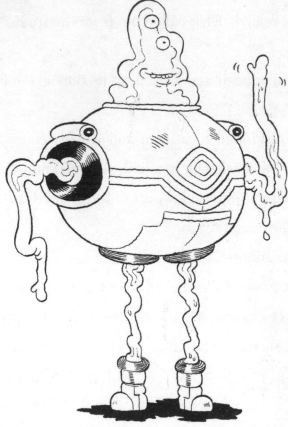

Tara and TJ were both pushing each other, trying to get a look outside. "Get out of the way!" she said.

"Let me see!" said TJ.

Kevin narrowed his eyes, peering out of his window. These aliens were roundish, oval-shaped creatures with soft, blob-like skin. They each had two arms and two legs, if you could even call them that. The limbs didn't seem to have joints. The aliens didn't look like they even had skeletons. They just sort of blobbed around, like washed-up jellyfish. Their uniforms looked like some kind of computerized smart suit that held their wobbling figures together.

One of the aliens only had one arm. A stream of blue-green fluid oozed from a stump at its shoulder, as if the arm had been blown off. Kevin watched as the alien's appendage slowly began to grow back, inch by inch, creating a new one where the missing limb had been.

"Yo, check it out," said Warner. "His arm's growing back!"

"What the heck are those things?" Tara asked. "I

feel like we should totally be hiding right now."

Klyk came over and looked out at the small group of gooey alien blobs. "It's okay. Those are the Glomms. They have the ability to regenerate if they get injured. This is their planet. They won't hurt us, but they're going to want some answers."

And maybe we'll get some of our own, too, Kevin thought.

The hatch doors slid open and two Glommian lieutenants stood in the doorframe. The Glomms gurgled orders for them to come out. Kevin, Warner, Tara, TJ, and Klyk stepped down into their twilit planet, and in an instant they were all hit with an awful stink.

"Oh my gosh," Warner said, hopping down behind Kevin. "What is that horrible smell?"

"Uck!" Tara pinched her nose, and TJ made an air mask with the collar of his T-shirt. "That's the worst thing ever!"

"It's just the way it smells here. You'll get used to it," Klyk said. "And stop talking about it. We 'aliens' can be very sensitive, too." He made quotation marks in the air around his head.

The commander of the Glomm platoon stepped forward. Its Jell-O-like mouth jabbered and a stream of grotesque sounds came out.

None of them had any idea what he was saying, except for Klyk.

Klyk raised his arms up in surrender and took one careful step toward the alien squadron. He flipped his language chip to a different setting and then uttered something in the gross-sounding alien language.

The aliens tapped a button on their smart suits, switching their language to English.

"Tell them we want to speak with their leader," Warner whispered to Klyk.

Klyk shushed him. "Let me handle this."

"We want to speak with your leader!" TJ spoke up.

"You are trespassers here," one of the Glomms said. "Now we will bring you to Narbok for questioning."

"See?" Warner said. "It works."

Kevin breathed in the alien stench and almost vomited on Tara as the Glommian soldiers approached them. He wasn't sure that he'd ever get used to it. He gagged and then breathed out, forcing himself not to throw up.

It's gonna be okay, he thought. *Mind over matter.*

Kevin and his friends dropped down onto the surface of the alien planet. The Glomm crew huddled around the humans. A Glommian soldier grasped Kevin by the arm. The Glomm's hands squished against Kevin's skin and left a wet, sticky mark, and then all of a sudden the alien locked both his wrists in high-tech shackles.

Uh-oh. Kevin hoped that these were really the good guys, and this was all a precaution. Otherwise, tracking down Max Greyson was going to be tougher than they thought.

Now captives, they trudged through the thick jungle. Kevin felt as small as a bug within the hugeness

of the landscape. Every tree trunk, every leaf, every flower was enormous. What looked like small townships hovered over the terrain. Walkways connected them thirty or forty feet above the ground. The Glomms ushered them into a metal elevator that rose up off the forested floor.

When they reached the treetops, Kevin could see a number of the walkways leading from the alien town to a vast mountain range peaking off the side of the planet's western hemisphere.

In silence, the Glomms escorted the five of them through a covered walkway high above the ground.

From there, they entered a large military command center with digital screens everywhere: control boards and mainframe computers, data displays, tactical computer readouts, and surveillance windows. Two dozen Glomms hustled and bustled every which way. On one of the main screens, there was a real-time radar display of the aerial warfare still raging outside the planet.

The Glommian general appeared in the doorway of the war room. He was twice as large and globular as any of his blob-like soldiers, and wore a high-tech armored suit, different from the others'.

The general clicked a button on his smart suit and spoke to Klyk in English. "I am General Narbok. What are you doing here with these Earthlings?" he asked.

Before Klyk could answer, Kevin jumped in and interrupted. "We're trying to find Max Greyson."

The alien general turned to Kevin. "Who gave you permission to speak?"

"I'm sorry to interrupt, sir, but we think the Sfinks have Max Greyson," Kevin said. "Do you know him?"

"Never heard of him," Narbok said. "Now you tell me what you know about the Sfinks."

"Like I said," said Kevin. "We think the Sfinks have Max Greyson."

"I don't care about Max Greyson!" Narbok roared. "The only thing that matters is keeping the crystals safe."

"Crystals?" Kevin asked, and twisted his face in confusion.

Just then one of the Glommian soldiers turned away

from the control panel and addressed his command-ing officer. "The Sfinks are entering our atmosphere, General," he said. "It's time."

Time? Kevin thought. *Time for what?*

General Narbok strutted to the center of the war room and gazed into a large, glowing orange crystal. A sphere of clear glass encased the gem, which was attached to a computer console and linked to the Glomms' high-tech equipment.

The general's eyeballs rolled into the back of his head as he studied the crystal intently for a few moments. "Blark-glark-phlark," Narbok said, then calmly ordered his crew of Glommian soldiers into action.

On one of the screens, Kevin could see another part of the battle. A whole group of black cruisers hovered just over the planet. A dozen Sfinks prepared to jump down onto the surface, but before they could take a step, a tremor shook the earth beneath them. Four of the Glommian drilling vehicles rose up out of the ground in a surprise attack. The Sfinks were blasted with some type of freeze-ray plasma before they even knew what hit them.

Kevin watched similar fights play out all across the planet, and the battle was over just as quickly as it had begun. He asked the general, "How did you know where they would attack you?"

"This is one of our crystals," Narbok said, pointing to the console at the center of the room. "The crystal shows us what's coming before it happens."

"You mean to tell us you have crystals that know the future?" Tara asked.

"Not all futures," Narbok replied. "But important events across time. Some events can't be allowed to happen or the universe will end."

"This battle, for example," Warner said, "must have been important."

"Very," said the Glomm general.

"Incoming!" Tara yelled, and gripped Kevin's arm with both hands.

All of a sudden the alien war room rumbled and the Glomms snapped to attention.

Two of the Sfinks' jet-black enemy cruisers swooped out of the sky over the Glomms' command center.

They were under attack.

The Sfinks' battle cruisers fired at the war room, and the photon blasts streaked toward them.

Two defense cannons fired up force-field shots that deflected the Sfinks' air strike well before it could do any damage.

The Sfinks' cruisers then zipped back up into the atmosphere as the Glomms' laser cannons shot across the sky.

General Narbok marched over to the crystal and smashed his gelatinous fist down on the console. "Blark!"

"What's the matter?" Kevin asked.

Narbok looked down at him. "This should not be happening. The Sfinks are getting too close. They're getting trickier. Like they know what we know and can alter their course." Narbok paused to collect himself. "I need to see the rest of the crystals. I can show them to you if you wish," Narbok said to the kids, raising what would have been an eyebrow.

"We definitely wish," Kevin said, a little overexcited, and then swallowed a nervous gulp.

"Follow me," the Glomm said. The alien blob led them to a hover pod located on the opposite side of the

war room. "But in return you must share what you know about the Sfinks and this Max Greyson."

The outer rim of the hover pod looked like an oversized inflatable life tube made out of shiny silver steel. An array of panels, handles, and vents detailed the aircraft's smooth silver metal exterior, and a curved glass hood covered the cockpit area. Under the bottom of the craft, three circular engines throbbed with an electromagnetic pulse.

They all hopped in the hover pod, and the vehicle launched off the airlocked docking station.

From the cockpit of the hover pod, Kevin could see in all directions. They glided through the air toward the mountain range. During the short flight, Narbok had a worried look on his face. The five of them all remained quiet as the alien mountain range grew closer and closer.

"Hey, Narbok." Warner eventually broke the silence. "You and your guys just destroyed those Sfinks. So what's the matter?"

"I am not happy that the Sfinks got two shots off at us," Narbok replied. He shook his head, eyes cast down. "Very troubling."

"Why?" TJ asked, pushing up his thick-lensed eyeglasses onto the bridge of his nose. "They weren't even close!"

"No one has ever gotten shots off inside our planet's atmosphere before, but since the Sfinks arrived, the crystals have been going a little haywire. If it hadn't been for your girlfriend here, we might all be dust."

"Well, you know, I do what I can," said Tara. "And just so you know, I'm not his girlfriend."

"I don't get it," Klyk said. "If you're having so much trouble with the Sfinks, why not call the IF?"

Narbok's gelatinous forehead crinkled into a glob that resembled an eyebrow. "You don't think we've tried?

The Sfinks have set up jamming satellites all around Gamma Major. All communications are being blocked. We've tried to take them out, but they're being heavily guarded."

The alien general then turned his head to look at Kevin and Tara. Well, his head didn't really turn. The neck just sort of twisted around and he was staring at them. "Now, what is this about the Sfinks and the one you call Max Greyson?"

"Back at our science camp on Earth, one of the Sfinks just appeared in this red light and stole our telepathy helmet," Kevin said. "Klyk tagged him with his little space tracker and we followed him here. They have Max Greyson, this really awesome comic book writer who got abducted by aliens. And now he can see the future. He sent us a message that the galaxy's in grave danger."

"Telepathy helmet . . . that must be how they are doing this." Narbok pondered this for a moment. "If the Sfinks somehow manage to take over this cave and access its powers, then the whole universe could be in big trouble. Whoever controls the crystals can control the future. And whoever controls the future controls everything. . . ."

They flew under a rocky arch and into a high-ceilinged cave where a massive deposit of crystals poked out of the stone walls. A light-blue glow came from the alien crystals and lit up the cave—all except one of the crystals, which gave off a bright orange light.

"What's that one over

there?" Klyk asked. "It's orange."

Narbok lowered the hover pod and parked it on the floor of the cave. Kevin waited for his friends to get out, then followed himself. His feet hit the ground, and Narbok turned to face them. "Blue means the projected future won't threaten the universe. Orange means something is out of whack and needs to be fixed."

Narbok's eyeballs rolled back into his blubbery jelly-like head, and he held his hands together at the thumbs as his other fingers fanned out like the feathers of a shadow-puppet bird. Kevin and his friends watched closely as Narbok slipped into some kind of trance. Soon the alien's hands began to generate some kind of energy and started to glow with a sparkling, pale-green light. The alien general aimed his powers at some of the blue crystals to show them the visions of the future.

Kevin's blood rushed with excitement as small 3-D holograms of events from all across the galaxy began to shine above the crystals. Each crystal was like a tiny movie projector, except these movies were actually happening, about to happen, or going to happen eventually.

"Holy cow!" TJ said, running his hand through the image projected into thin air. "These things are going on right now?"

"Hey, look!" Tara said pointing to one of the crystals. "That's Mim!"

Kevin squinted through his glasses and focused on

the projection. Mim, the little alien fur ball who tried to eat planet Earth less than two days ago, was behind bars in a jail cell. The cell was made of arachnopod silk, the only known substance that the little alien mercenary couldn't chew through. Their former friend, now an intragalactic prisoner, was guarded by space cops, and he didn't look too happy about it.

Narbok grimaced at Mim's image. "That alien's bad," he said. "Like these two." He aimed his hands at a nearby crystal, and Kevin's eyes bulged as Zouric and Nuzz appeared in the air. They were the two aliens who had tried to enslave every human on Earth only hours before. The big slug-like alien and the little robotic brain alien held each other, like frightened teenagers in a horror film. Their former enemies were walking through dangerous terrain, a thick, dark forest with alien monsters popping out of the shadows.

"That's Zouric and Nuzz!" Warner shouted excitedly.

Narbok gave him a funny look. "You know these two?"

"Do we know them?" Warner said. "Heck yeah, we do! We wormholed their butts across the galaxy before they could take over our planet."

"That was you?" Narbok asked, sounding impressed. "We wondered who did that."

"I watched them do it," Klyk said.

"Can we look at the orange one?" Kevin asked, pointing away from the blue crystals.

"That one just turned orange," the alien general said, walking up a pathway carved out in the cave's steep walls. The four science campers and Klyk followed the Glomm leader.

Narbok aimed his hands at the orange crystal, and a 3-D image appeared above the rock formation. The two aliens in the hologram looked vaguely familiar. It took Kevin a second, but then he remembered. It was Phirf and Drooq, the two alien bounty hunters they had zapped with the wormhole generator.

Klyk gasped and let out an electronic hiss. "Those are my friends!"

In the crystal's vision of a possible future, Phirf and Drooq were lying unconscious in the dirt. Then, as if pulled down by quicksand, the two aliens disappeared into the ground.

"Whoa!" Warner said. "Did that just happen?"

"No," Narbok said. "But it will if we don't do something. It will."

"Where are they?" Klyk asked, his voice a bit frantic.

"Planet Dybunk—that looks like their terrain," Narbok told them. "Not too far from here."

"I bet I know where they are!" said Klyk. "They're at the Mooymallo!"

"The what?" Tara said.

"The Moo-E-Mall-Oh," Klyk repeated slowly. "It's a saloon. Or a roadhouse. Like a hangout for alien tough guys."

"Like cowboys in a Western?" Warner asked. "Or like truckers at a truck stop?"

"A little bit of both," Klyk said.

"You must go to the Mooymallo on Planet Dybunk and rescue these two," Narbok said. "They've upset the crystals. They must be saved."

Kevin nodded. Phirf and Drooq couldn't be

abandoned. Plus, they were experts on the Sfinks. Without Phirf and Drooq, the kids—and the Glomms—didn't stand a chance. "We'll get you a new spaceship for your journey. But the Glomms stay here and defend the crystals—it's too dangerous for us to leave the crystals unguarded. After you pick up your friends and rescue Max, you have to come back here to help us fight the Sfinks."

"Mission accepted," Warner said, and the four kids gave each other a knowing glance. They had already saved the world twice. Why not go for a third?

The Glomm general bounded back toward the hover pod. Kevin ran after the Jell-O-like alien, along with TJ, Tara, and Klyk. Kevin stopped halfway to the craft and turned around. Warner was nowhere in sight.

"Warner!" Kevin shouted back for his buddy.

After a second, Warner's voice called back. "Yo!"

"What are you doing?"

"I'm just exploring a little bit," Warner yelled.

"No time for that, man," Kevin shouted impatiently. "We gotta get outta here!"

"All right! I'm comin', I'm comin'." Warner appeared, jogging out from behind a big rock formation. He caught up to Kevin and they both jumped onto the hover pod before Narbok hit the gears.

The pod levitated off the floor of the cave and swooped back toward the military headquarters of planet Glomm.

Everyone was quiet on the ride back to the war room. Kevin was lost in thought. They couldn't let the Sfinks get control of that cave. But if the Glomms were

the only ones who could see the crystals, then how did the Sfinks expect to control the future? Kevin had no idea what the Sfinks had up their sleeves, but Max had something to do with it. He had a feeling they would find out soon, for better or worse. But first they had to find Phirf and Drooq. They needed all the help they could get if they were going to find Max Greyson and stop the Sfinks.

Narbok guided their hover pod back to the air-locked dock. The general bounced out of the pod and slunk into the war room, shouting orders at his soldiers in the Glommian tongue.

"What are they saying?" Tara asked.

TJ listened to the alien language as Narbok continued to gargle orders to his troops.

"I think he's saying to get the starship ready. . . . ," TJ said.

"How do you know that?" Kevin asked.

"Yeah, how do you know that?" Klyk asked.

"They speak in a simple language of five different noises with different intonations, which in combination form various meanings," he told them. "Kind of like Chinese, but way simpler."

"You're just making that up to sound smart!" Warner said to him.

"Why would I do that?" TJ asked. "I am smart."

"Look!" Kevin said, pointing out the huge window. His friends turned to look at a large metallic spacecraft as it rose into view.

The spaceship was sleek, with the overall shape of a trapezoid. It was relatively flat, like a stealth bomber, though it had some bulk from all the weapons attached to the wings and under the hull. It was the same silver metal as the other Glomm ships, but the metal was scuffed and a little rusted around the edges. But it was still an impressive vessel, and Kevin was filled with a tingly thrill of excitement.

Warner gazed up in awe at the Glommian warship.

"Don't even think about it," Klyk said and stepped in front of Warner, blocking his view of the ship. With a salute to the general, he walked down to the loading dock.

Kevin turned to Narbok. "Thank you for helping us."

"Don't thank me yet," Narbok said. "I'll thank you after you help us beat the Sfinks."

"Let's go, Kev!" TJ said, waving from the loading dock.

"I have to go," Kevin said to Narbok. "But the next

time you see us we'll be with Max Greyson. And we'll help you defeat the Sfinks. I promise!"

Oops, Kevin thought. Usually he didn't promise things he wasn't sure about, but did it really matter? If they didn't rescue Max, then the next time he saw Narbok would be never.

About half an hour later, the Glomms' space cruiser descended through the atmosphere of planet Dybunk, home of the Mooymallo saloon. The extraterrestrial sky was orange-red with thick, dark gray clouds swooshing quickly through the air.

"Here we are," Klyk said as they landed. The spaceship's engine went quiet. "The Mooymallo is right over there." The cyborg pointed at a modest-looking roadhouse about a hundred yards off.

Kevin glanced out the spaceship's window. It looked like they were smack in the middle of a desert. There were no trees or plant life. Nothing green, only dunes of dark brown dirt for miles.

Warner pressed the button to unlock the exit hatch, and Kevin, TJ, Tara, and Klyk all jumped down to the dirty ground. Kevin breathed in the alien air. It was thick and hard to suck in through his nose, like trying to breathe through a drinking straw.

Kevin's chest tightened and he reached for his inhaler. He felt around in his pocket, but it wasn't there. All he could feel was the laser pointer, which he kept with him almost always. He was starting to panic when TJ stepped up next to him and handed him the inhaler.

"I snagged it before we left Earth," TJ said. "Thought you might need it."

Kevin let out a sigh of relief and smiled at his friend. "Thanks, Teej." He put the inhaler to his mouth and took a puff. Much better.

He took a step forward and felt his leg take a bigger step than he intended. He tried to push off his back leg but wound up in a painful split position that sent a pang through his groin muscle.

"Help," Kevin uttered in a high-pitched squeal.

Klyk appeared next to him and helped him back up.

"Whoa!" said Warner as he bounded down from the spacecraft, hit the ground with his feet, and then jumped four feet up in the air like it was nothing.

"Gravity's a little bit different here," Klyk informed them. "So be careful. Take it slow."

TJ took a running start and leaped as far as he could. He gracefully floated in the air for about ten yards, spreading his arms like a ballet dancer in slow motion, before making a perfect landing.

"Nice move, Teej," said Tara. "Check this out!" She hopped off one foot and flew straight up in the air. She spun her body around and around, like a figure skater doing the toughest trick in the book.

"This place is amazing!" Kevin said.

"Don't get carried away," Klyk said to them. "We still

have to find my friends."

Klyk trudged through the terrain toward the road-house. Kevin focused on keeping his feet on the ground and walking normally, stepping into the giant footprints Klyk left behind. He looked up as they approached the alien saloon. All types of land cruisers were parked in front of the structure, like so many rows of motorcycles outside a biker bar. At least two dozen hover pods and spaceships levitated around the alien establishment.

"After you," Klyk said, and pushed open the door.

Warner strolled through first, trying to look super-cool. Kevin entered next, surprised by the spaciousness of the room. It didn't make sense. Outside, the place looked so small, but inside it had the dimensions of a large warehouse.

The alien nightclub was packed. There was music in the air that sounded like a mix of jazz and hip-hop. Kevin looked around and noticed a group of aliens strumming instruments on a large bandstand. The melody was poppy and electronic. The bass line and beat were kind of funky. It sounded pretty good.

Tara bobbed her head to the beat as they walked through the crowd.

Behind her, TJ tried to keep a low profile. He looked nervous. "I'm not sure this was such a good idea," he said.

"Chill out, TJ," Warner said. "Act like you've been here before."

The alien roadhouse was packed with all kinds of extraterrestrial weirdoes, outlaws, and the like. Almost every type of alien in the galaxy was in attendance. There were humanoids and insectoids, reptilians and mammalians. There were walking, talking things that looked like they came from the bottom of the ocean. There were little green men with tiny eye slits and no nose, just two nostrils and a small mouth. There were taller gray men with big, wide eyes, jet black and glossy.

"Let's sit and have a drink," Klyk said. "They have the best fizzers in the whole galaxy here."

"What's a fizzer?" Tara asked.

"It's like what you would call a soda pop, but it gives you a little burst of energy," Klyk told them as he led

them to an empty table. They all sat down, but Kevin was anxious. He didn't want a fizzer. He wanted to find Phirf and Drooq and get the heck out of here.

"I know we just got here, guys," he said. "But I don't think we have time to hang around."

"Relax," Klyk said. "I know one of the waiters. His name is Vilborg. He'll know if Phirf and Drooq have been here."

"What do they look like again?" Kevin asked, trying to calm his nerves a little.

Klyk pulled out his hologram device and brought up a picture of both his friends. Phirf's face was like a squid, with one eye and a beard of little wormlike tentacles. His neck sprouted out of a short, squat robotic computer body with three squiggly, boneless arms, one of which held a photon blaster. He stood on two mechanical legs that bent backward at the knee joint.

Drooq was a hideous-looking crab-legged slug beast. He had two eyeballs stuck to the ends of two antennae that came out of the sides of his head where the temples would be. His torso was the shape of a slug, and the whole top of his head was one big mouth.

"They don't exactly blend in, do they?" Tara commented.

"That's what I'm saying," Kevin said. "I think we should go look for them."

"I don't know, man," Warner said. "There are some pretty freaky-looking dudes in here. Just wait a minute. I want to try a fizzer."

"Me, too," TJ said. "I'm dying of thirst!"

"Vilborg!" Klyk called jovially across the bar. "Get on over here!"

A computerized-sounding voice called back. "Klyk!"

He was *definitely* one weird-looking dude.

The extraterrestrial waiter came over to their table on his three robot legs. He had four thick tentacles for arms and had five eyes wrapping around his cone-shaped head. Three antennae sprouted out of a funny-looking haircut, which was shaped like the fronds of a palm tree. His four tentacle arms were also covered in some kind of thick, matted, slime-slickened fur.

"Long time, old friend!" Vilborg said, sidling up to

their table. "You speaking English now?"

"It's more for these four than anything else," Klyk said, gesturing to Kevin and his friends.

"Hey, kids, welcome to the Mooymallo!" Vilborg said. "You look like you could use a few fizzers. Let me get you started."

Vilborg's tentacle arms reached inside a compartment in the bottom of his robot lower half and produced five glasses of a fizzy drink, setting them down on the table in front of Klyk and the kids. The drinks were dark green and very fizzy, with some kind of steam rising off the surface, like a beaker full of chemicals in a mad scientist's laboratory.

"Got another question for you, too, Vilborg," Klyk said to his alien buddy. "You seen two of my guys around here lately?" He showed him the picture of Phirf and Drooq.

Vilborg squinted all five of his eyes at the hologram, then made a face. "I haven't seen them, but I just started my shift . . . sorry. I'll ask around."

"Thanks, Vilborg," Klyk said.

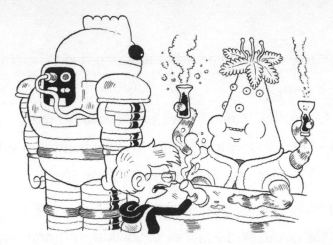

TJ leaned over the table and wafted some of the steam toward his nose as if he were sniffing a caustic mixture in chemistry class. "Smells all right," he said and lifted the drink to his lips.

Klyk did the same and so did Warner and Tara and Kevin, swigging back the alien fizzer drinks. Klyk finished his whole mug in a single gulp, but Kevin could barely take a tiny sip. It tasted like freshly mown grass mixed with dog poop. He spat it out on the floor and looked around at his friends, who were enjoying their fizzers.

"Are you guys kidding me?" Kevin looked shocked as his friends guzzled down their drinks. "This stuff tastes like dog doo!"

"How do you know what dog doo-doo tastes like?" Tara asked.

"Actually, I should have mentioned it before," said Klyk. "A fizzer tastes different to everybody, depending on your mood and your emotional output. If you're happy, it tastes delicious. If you're cranky, it tastes horrible."

"Mine tastes like marshmallows and gummi bears!" Warner said. "I must be in a great mood!"

"Me, too!" TJ said. "I'll have another round."

"Me, three!" Tara said.

Klyk raised his hand and snapped his fingers at Vilborg, who was across the saloon. Their furry cyborg waiter nodded and gave them the universal sign for "just a second."

"Well, I'm obviously not in the mood for these drinks," Kevin said, grabbing Klyk's hologram device and hopping out of his seat. "I'm gonna go see if any of these alien dudes have seen Phirf and Drooq."

Klyk reached out his arm, and it thunked Kevin in the chest. "Just be careful," he said. "Most of these characters aren't the nicest guys in the galaxy."

"Relax and drink your fizzers," Kevin said, brushing past him. "Let me handle this."

Kevin strolled through the crowd. A lot of the aliens were much taller than him, and so he only came up to their waists. He shuffled around four alien butts, tall, lanky, thin, and glowing faintly with some kind of life-force energy. They looked like aliens he had seen in the movies back on Earth.

"Excuse me," he said to them, cocking his neck back. "Have you seen these aliens?"

The spindly beings shook their heads no, and Kevin moved on to the next ones.

Three small alien mammalians stopped in front of Kevin, who was still holding up the 3-D hologram. They looked like tiny monkeys, pygmy marmosets to be exact, but walking on their hind legs and standing a little shorter than Kevin.

"Have you seen these aliens?"

One of the furry little pygmies belched and blew his stinky breath in Kevin's face. The trio sauntered off without so much as a word to Kevin.

"That was rude!" he said, backing away from the lingering stink of the alien burp.

Kevin knocked into a table and spun around to apologize. The seats were empty, but the table still had drinks on it. Something moved behind one of the cups, and Kevin gasped as a disgusting little critter scampered across the tabletop. It had a round, fat body segmented into three sections. It had six legs and feet like suction cups, and its eyeballs extended from two feelers on the side of its head that probed the air in front of its face.

Kevin stuck out his index finger and slowly went to pet the alien with his fingertip.

It was almost cute-looking, until it opened its tiny little mouth to reveal three rows of sharp, jagged teeth, and then sunk those teeth into Kevin's finger.

"Yow!" Kevin howled and grabbed an empty glass off the table. The little alien critter backed up as Kevin brought the glass upside down over its head with a clunk.

The slimy critter shrieked with unbelievable volume, almost shrill enough to break the glass around it. Kevin held the glass on top of it, but it could almost chew through the cup.

Just then two humongous thugs stomped over to the table.

They both looked at Kevin. Neither one of them looked happy. The first one had the body of an armless

man, with a mutant octopus that sat on top of the armless man's head, like a hat. The octo-man's tentacles dangled around his shoulders. The other hooligan looked like Bigfoot on steroids, just a woolly mammoth of muscle and fur.

"I'm sorry to bother you fellas. There was a really gross bug crawling on your table," Kevin said and started to show them the picture of Phirf and Drooq.

The alien duo towered over Kevin, each one over seven feet high. They grilled him with their fearsome eyes, looking down, saying nothing.

"Really sorry," Kevin said to their unblinking faces. "I'm just trying to find a couple friends of mine. . . ."

He held up the hologram photo and the octo-man's tentacle shot out, wrapping around Kevin's neck. The slimy tentacle arm lifted Kevin off the floor. His feet dangled, and Klyk's device clattered to the ground. The tentacle tightened.

"Human, that really gross bug is our pet. . . ."

Kevin was choking, losing air. He tried to call for help, but no sound came out. He felt his eyes popping out of their sockets. If this alien freak squeezed his neck any harder he thought his brain might explode, which would be bad news, well, because he'd grown rather attached to it.

Out of the corner of his bulging eyeball, Kevin caught a glimpse of Klyk as he stepped into view. "Drop him!" Klyk ordered the two goons.

The alien turned to Klyk and let out something that resembled a laugh. The musclebound Bigfoot chuckled as well. The octo-alien's tentacle retracted, and Kevin fell to the floor.

The alien hip-hop jazz band played on.

Kevin gasped for air and looked up as both aliens charged at Klyk. The cyborg made a move to block them, but they picked him up and slammed him down on the table.

A loud crash sounded and drinks flew off the table-top, splattering fizzy liquid across the floor.

Warner, TJ, and Tara ran over, pushing through

the alien riffraff. Warner and TJ grabbed Kevin under his arms and pulled him to his feet. Tara turned to the two aliens, who were holding Klyk down on the table. She raised both arms at them and yelled, "Freeze!" Her hands were clutching the freeze ray, her finger on the trigger button.

In a flash the octo-man lashed out a tentacle and snatched the freeze ray right out of her hands.

"Hey! Give that back!"

The Bigfoot-looking alien reeled around and grabbed Tara by the shirt collar. The hairy beast raised his arm and lifted her at least ten feet off the ground.

"Put her down!"

Kevin heard a reptilian voice call out.

"And let him go!" Another reptilian voice shouted at the octo-man.

Kevin also heard the electromagnetic sound of two ray guns charging up.

"Whoa, man," said TJ. "It's the Kamilions!"

Just yesterday, Kevin and his friends had saved the Kamilions from Zouric and Nuzz back on Earth. The

Kamilions owed them and promised to protect them if they were ever in danger. They were good aliens to have on your side.

Kevin smiled as the octo-man and Bigfoot let go of Klyk and Tara.

"Get out of here," one of the Kamilions said, training his laser ray on the alien hoodlums as they stepped back from the fight.

"They really do have our backs!" Warner said.

"Humans and Kamilions are friends and allies," the Kamilion told them. "Our reptilian kind will never forget what you did for us on Earth."

"Yeah, get lost!" TJ shouted at the octo-man and his furry buddy with a bit too much energy. "And stay lost!"

The Kamilions helped Klyk up, and the boys helped Tara to her feet.

"Everybody all right?" the first Kamilion asked them.

"Yeah, we're good," Tara said, brushing herself off.

The second Kamilion turned to Klyk. "What are you doing here with these four? The Mooymallo isn't a place for children."

"I know that," Klyk said. "We're looking for my friends. . . ."

Kevin stepped forward and showed them the picture of Phirf and Drooq. The Kamilions studied the aliens in the 3-D photo.

"Yeah, they were here about half an hour ago," the first Kamilion told them.

"Really?" Kevin sounded excited.

"That's right," said the second Kamilion. "They were trying to hitch a ride with some Flumps to their home planet. Not a good idea if you ask me. Flumps can't be trusted."

"Can you two help us?" Kevin asked.

"We would, but we're scheduled to take off in a few minutes," the other Kamilion said. "Sorry."

"Did they say where they were going?" Klyk asked.

"I overheard them saying they were headed to the Dunes," said the first Kamilion.

"Klyk, do you know where that is?"

"Yeah, but why are they going all the way over

there?" he asked, sounding worried.

The Kamilions both shrugged. "Like we said, the Flumps are usually up to no good. But if you do run into them, don't let them spit at you. Their spit is like poison. It'll burn your skin right off."

Klyk turned to the kids. "We gotta hurry. If they hitch a ride with the Flumps and leave the planet, we might not be able to find them before it's too late."

A few miles away from the Mooymallo saloon, Kevin climbed to the top of a giant dune and dug his hands into the grimy soil. Black extraterrestrial dirt was packed under his fingernails.

At the top of the hill, Kevin looked down and noticed something wriggling in the black soil. He plucked at it, pulling up a red-and-purple-colored worm with a tiny little mouth and tiny little teeth. Klyk had warned them about these things on the way here. He called them dune worms, and he also said they could get pretty big.

Kevin was on the lookout. He knew now the dune worms were the ones responsible for sucking Phirf and Drooq into the ground in the crystal vision, and Kevin didn't want to get sucked down himself.

Far below, the Flumps' space shuttle hovered just above the ground. Phirf and Drooq knelt in the dirt, the Flumps surrounding them. They had both been disarmed, with their weapons lying at the feet of their alien captors. There seemed to be about three or four ray guns, a high-tech sword, and some kind of long battle-ax in the pile. The Flumps had stolen everything.

The Flumps looked disgusting. They were by far the ugliest type of alien Kevin had ever seen. They had furry white manes and beards, with long, dangly mustaches that draped down on either side of their long, sharp fangs. Each had four eyeballs attached to antennae on top of their heads. They had three separate snouts drooping out of the middle of their faces, like an elephant would if it had three trunks.

The Flumps also had only one leg, which they used to hop and bounce around. On its own, a Flump leg looked like a rhinoceros's hoof.

Kevin didn't like the look of them. Not one bit.

Klyk was positioned on the other side of the dirt hill, about a hundred yards off. Behind the crest of a dune to Kevin's left, Tara and TJ were getting ready to ambush the Flumps and help Phirf and Drooq escape.

The plan was to wait for Klyk's first move. In a matter of seconds, he would shoot off a few warning shots. When the Flumps fired back at Klyk's dune, Kevin, Tara, and TJ would attack from behind. Warner finally got his chance to pilot their spacecraft, which he was extremely excited about. He was ready to swoop down once they had rescued Phirf and Drooq.

Kevin was armed with a freeze ray, and Tara had one as well. TJ was manning the shrink ray.

PYOO! PYOO!

Klyk fired the opening shots, and the one-legged Flumps spun around on their hooves. Their elephantine trunks rose up like trumpets. They all aimed at Klyk's dune.

Kevin looked to his left and saw Tara charging down

the hill. She was very quick in the low gravity, covering over twenty or even thirty feet with each running step.

The Flumps fired a bunch of slimy balls from their trunks up into the air. Klyk disappeared on the other side of the dune. The snot rockets arced up and landed in the middle of the dirt hill, slicing through it. The dune collapsed in on itself, and an avalanche of soil sank down about a hundred feet.

TJ remained at the top of the hill, lining up the Flumps' spacecraft in the sight of the shrink ray.

Kevin ran down the dune, too, leaping into the air

and charging at the backs of the Flumps.

TJ hit the target on the screen and the shrink ray flashed, sending a ray beam toward the Flumps' ship.

Zap!

The large space vessel appeared to vanish as it shrunk down to the size of some plastic toy.

At the top of his dune, TJ pumped his fist and made a whooping sound as Kevin raced to get a closer angle to take down the Flumps. He leaped into the air, his freeze ray ready to shoot.

The Flumps hopped around to face Kevin and fired

their acidic saliva straight at him. Kevin fired at the blobs of alien slobber. The freeze ray stopped the disgusting blitz. The mucus-y missiles hardened in midair and dropped to the ground with a thump.

Kevin landed and somersaulted over the rest of the Flumps' lethal spitballs.

Flump-flump-flump-flump-flump!

The Flumps kept attacking with their poisoned wads of spittle. It was raining alien saliva, each ball about the size and volume of a bowlful of macaroni and cheese.

ZAP! ZAP!

Tara fired two shots from her freeze ray, and two of the aliens stiffened in place and toppled onto their sides like tipped-over statues.

The gang of Flumps spread out, hopping and bounding on their single-legged bodies, hawking loogies in rapid succession.

Tara jumped up to dodge the Flumps' attack, and a glob of spittle struck the shrunken spaceship behind her. The miniaturized spacecraft sizzled and started to bubble and melt.

Kevin dove to his right and rolled in the dirt, dodging another blast. He shot his freeze ray and tagged a Flump right on its kneecap, freezing the one-legged beast before it could blow another snot rocket his way.

"Watch out!" someone yelled behind him.

Kevin spun around and saw that a steaming-hot spatter of Flump juice was coming right at him.

OOPH!

Kevin tumbled as someone tackled him from the side.

"Ahhhhhh!"

Kevin groaned as he rolled under the weight of his giant rescuer. He picked up his head and found himself staring directly into Drooq's grotesque slug face.

"You!" The mouth on top of Drooq's head moved as he spoke. "You're the one that got us into this mess in the first place!"

"Sorry about that." Kevin shrugged sheepishly. "We're with Klyk now. We're here to rescue you!"

"You rescue me?" Drooq scoffed. "Ha!"

A batch of alien spittle flew through the air behind Drooq's head, and Kevin's reflexes took over. He fired the freeze ray again and the snot rocket fell to the ground.

"Nice shot!" Drooq said in a deep, rough voice, like he was trying to gargle mouthwash and talk at the same time.

Kevin and Drooq scrambled to their feet and headed toward their getaway ship.

Dirt flew off the hilltop as their spaceship cruised over the dune. Kevin watched TJ jump into the air, grab onto the edge of the hatch, and climb aboard the craft.

"Come on!" Kevin yelled to Drooq, and they both bolted toward the dune.

The Flumps bounded after them. For one-legged aliens, they were surprisingly fast.

Kevin looked to his right and saw Klyk, Tara, and Phirf in full sprint, heading for their spaceship, too. The three of them blasted away with their weapons, shooting at the Flumps, who threw their sticky spitballs in response.

The spaceship swooped over the dune's peak and stopped above them. There was no time to land. The

Flumps were too close.

"Get in!" TJ yelled, his head peeking down from up above.

Phirf hopped up with ease. His robot legs propelled him in the air and he was in. Drooq jumped up next, followed by Klyk, who leaned down and reached his strong arm down to help Kevin and Tara.

Kevin looked at her, while tagging one of the Flumps with a blast from the freeze ray. Tara jumped up next and clasped onto Klyk's outstretched arm.

Kevin tried to hurdle skyward. He soared up toward the spaceship but was jerked backward.

Something had him by the ankle.

He looked down and saw a dune worm stretching up out of the soil. It was wrapped around his leg, pulling him down.

"Kevin!" Tara screamed his name, reaching out her hand.

The Flumps were coming, snorting their snot ammo at him. Kevin didn't know what to do. He had to think quickly. He couldn't freeze the thing, or he'd risk being frozen himself. The incoming spit-slime streaked through the air, ready to burn him to death. Kevin felt his problem-solving skills kick in and all he could do was react.

He bent his knees and jumped up as high as he could.

He soared up and the alien earthworm stretched out. He leveled off just above the snot rockets and they seared through the worm's flesh, freeing his ankle.

The band of Flumps gathered underneath, ready to end him if he fell. Kevin halted a little in the air and flailed his arms. He was almost at the open hatch, reaching for Klyk's helping hand, but he was going to fall short.

The spaceship made a sudden dip and lowered. Kevin was now only inches from Klyk, who stretched out his arm and grabbed Kevin in his mighty grip.

"Gotcha!" Klyk yelled and pulled him into the ship.

The Flumps tried to jump up, too, but couldn't quite reach. They were just shy of Kevin's feet.

Warner hit the thrusters and the spaceship took off,

leaving
the nasty
crew of alien sickos
far behind and Kevin
safely in the clutches of
Klyk.

Kevin sat on the floor of the Glommian spaceship while Warner steered them through the vast black infinity of space.

"Get it off me!" Kevin yelled. "Get it off me!" He tugged at the alien worm that was still wrapped around his ankle. But the worm squeezed tighter the harder Kevin pulled. Even though it had been cut in half, it was alive and stronger than ever.

Phirf looked down at him and said calmly, "Better get rid of that thing before you lose a foot."

Kevin looked at Klyk's alien partner and raised two worried eyebrows.

"Here you go," said Drooq. "Let me help." The alien

pulled out a large knife and expertly sliced into the worm with the blade. The dune worm split in two and fell off Kevin's leg onto the floor.

Kevin breathed easy and watched as Drooq picked up the severed worm and popped it into his giant head-mouth. He chewed and chewed the tough wormy meat, and TJ's stomach flipped in disgust.

"I think I'm gonna be sick," TJ said.

"That was some pretty fancy flying," Phirf said.

Warner tipped an invisible hat. "Just doing what I do best."

Klyk towered over Warner, who was still sitting in the pilot's seat. "Out . . ."

"Even after that?" Warner said, throwing up his hands in disbelief.

Klyk nodded and Warner gave over the controls. Klyk sat down and put the ship on autopilot. "What were you two doing?" he asked Phirf and Drooq. "Don't you know better than to go hitching rides with a bunch of Flumps?"

"We were trying to get back to you," Drooq said. "We thought you were in trouble."

"We didn't have any choice but to trust the Flumps," Phirf said. "All communication is down in this part of the galaxy. Nobody seems to know why."

"We know why," Kevin said. "It's the Sfinks."

"Sfinks?" Drooq said. "We should call this in to the IF."

"We can't," Klyk said. "The Sfinks are blocking all communication signals trying to come out of the star system."

"Oh! Now it makes sense why we couldn't get backup just now," Drooq realized. "We tried to signal for help, and then we got lucky when you showed up."

"Forget about that, let's get down to business," Warner said. "What do you know about the Sfinks?"

"Whoa, Klyk, your new friends really don't waste any time," Drooq said, chuckling out of his mouth-head.

"Just answer the question, Drooq," Tara said. "We don't exactly know how much time we have. . . ." She tapped a make-believe watch on her wrist.

"Let me guess." Drooq looked down at Tara. "You're the feisty one."

"The Sfinks have been around for a long time. They have highly advanced technology," Phirf said. "They're kind of like space pirates. They hijack. They kidnap. They steal. They think they're better than everybody else."

"Where do they come from?"

"It's been said that the Sfinks destroyed their own planet and they live on a massive space station that's also an aircraft carrier for their entire fleet. They zoom around the galaxy, popping up wherever and whenever they want to, stealing precious resources until they can find a new home. Although now it looks like they're trying to take over the whole galaxy." Phirf looked around at Kevin and the gang. "What do you need to know about the Sfinks for anyway? It's better not to get involved with them."

"We don't have a choice," Kevin said. "The Glomms are under attack from the Sfinks. The Sfinks want to take over their planet because of this cave that's filled with these crystals that tell the future of the galaxy. . . ."

"Hold on a second," Phirf said. "Did you just say planet Glomm?"

"Yeah, we were just there," Warner said. "And it was sick!"

"You mean the planet's dying?" Phirf asked.

"No, I mean it was *cool*," Warner said to Drooq's blank stare, then shook his head.

"You mean cold?" Drooq replied.

"Never mind," Warner said.

"We went to their planet and they showed us their cave," Tara said.

"That's impossible," Drooq said. "No one visits planet Glomm. The IF cut off all travel after its discovery before the Quasar Wars."

"You know about the cave?" Klyk asked.

"I mean, I've heard about it," Phirf said, "But I thought it was just a fairy tale. Until now."

"What do you mean, fairy tale?" Warner asked.

"Everyone I know thinks the cave is just a myth," Phirf continued. "The Glomms are the only aliens that live on the planet, and honestly, no one ever wanted to go there because it smells so bad. But rumor had it that a cave of crystals that could predict the future lay at the center of the planet and the Glomms were sworn to protect it. The crystals are said to foretell events that show the possible fates of the galaxy."

"Supposedly, the IF gives the Glomms everything they need to protect the crystals, as long as the Glomms report back to them with any threats to the galaxy. They give the Glomms spaceships, weapons, technology, and special air defense artillery. In return, the Glomms give them all the intelligence about the future they need to stop anything dangerous to galactic security. So as long as the Glomms have control of the future-telling crystals and the means to stop an attack . . . then it's impossible for anyone to get past them. Even the Sfinks," Phirf finished.

"That's not true anymore," Klyk jumped in. "The Sfinks are getting closer. They seem to have a way to get to the crystals."

"Even still," Phirf said. "According to the myth, the Glomms are the only ones who can visualize the crystals because of their biological makeup."

"Have you ever heard of Max Greyson?" Kevin asked the two bounty hunters. Drooq and Phirf both shook their heads.

Kevin then turned to Warner. "Show them the comic book. . . ."

Warner pulled the Max Greyson comic book out from his bag and flipped it open to the warning message in the final pages.

Drooq and Phirf examined the plea for help. Drooq's antennae eyeballs waggled back and forth, scanning left to right as he read.

"We received it through a transmitter, after we took down Zouric and Nuzz," replied Warner.

"You took down Zouric and Nuzz?" Phirf asked, sounding impressed.

"Yeah, but now we have to rescue Max from the Sfinks before they take over the Glomms' crystal cave, and then the galaxy!" said Kevin.

Phirf turned to Drooq and shot his partner a worried look. "How do you even know that the Sfinks have this Max fellow?"

"We got this hidden message in the comic book, and then one of the Sfinks came to Earth and stole our telepathy helmet," said Tara.

"Yeah," Kevin added. "And we tracked the Sfink and he was going to the same coordinates as Max."

"So why do the Sfinks want some comic book writer from Earth?" said Drooq.

"That we're not sure about," Kevin said, "but we think they're using him to infiltrate planet Glomm."

"Why would Max Greyson be able to help them with that?"

"We think that for whatever reason, he has the power to predict events that will happen, too. They might be using Max's psychic abilities to mess with the Glomms' crystals," Kevin said.

"Wait, back up," Phirf said. "How do you have a telepathy helmet?"

"Had," Tara corrected. "We got it from Mim. But the Sfinks took it."

"Mim," said Drooq. "What ever happened to that little fur ball?"

"We blasted him back to space prison," Warner said, a cocky smirk curling up at the corner of his lip.

"If you kids keep this up, you're going to put us out

of a job," said Drooq.

"If the Sfinks have a telepathy helmet, then . . ." Phirf paused and looked at Drooq.

"Then what?" Kevin asked.

"Then they could actually pull off a hostile takeover of planet Glomm . . . ," Phirf said.

"How can they do that?" Klyk asked his bounty hunter buddy.

"It's complicated, but if Max has some psychic pow- ers already, then the helmet could amplify his neural path- ways and he could interfere with the crystals' power to tell the future."

"That's true," Kevin said, scratching his chin. "Once some- body knows what the future is going to be, they can change it. Max is probably throwing the whole thing out of whack."

"I'm starting to feel like you

want us to get in the middle of this," Phirf said. "I don't think that's a good idea."

"Terrible idea," Drooq agreed. "We've gone up against some Sfinks before. And it's not something we ever want to do again,"

"Well, the crystals said we needed to find you." Klyk sighed with disappointment. "But I guess if you're not up for it . . ."

"Don't get cocky on us, Klyk. Remember who got you out of the Nebula Riots in one piece," Phirf said.

"Come on, you guys," Kevin pleaded. "The fate of the galaxy is in jeopardy. We need you. The crystals even said so!"

"All right, all right, but you have to realize that it's not going to be easy," Drooq said. "These guys are way tougher than Mim or even Zouric and Nuzz. They don't mess around."

"Yup, those guys are really good at being bad!" said Phirf.

Kevin's eyes narrowed and his voice took on a serious tone. "Well, we're really bad at being good."

"Umm," TJ said. "That doesn't really make sense."

"Unless you meant bad like the good way," Tara said. "But that's still confusing."

"She's right. You should have said something like . . ." Warner paused and thought for a moment. "Well, we're really good at being awesome."

"Yeah, that would've sounded much cooler," Klyk agreed, and Phirf and Drooq nodded their heads yes.

"Whatever," Kevin sighed. "Let's just go show these nasty feline alien thugs exactly what we're made of."

"What?" TJ looked up, his eyebrows crinkled in confusion. "Mostly water?"

Kevin shook his head. "Time to rescue Max and stop the Sfinks!"

"Here we go." Klyk turned off the ship's autopilot, taking over the controls.

"Make a hard right toward Dybunk's outer moon," Phirf told his friend. "There's a wormhole shortcut we can take back to Glomm's star system faster."

"Check those coordinates from the tracker again," Drooq said.

"On it," Klyk said, hitting the thrusters.

In a flash, their spaceship banked to the right, veering off toward the wormhole back to planet Glomm.

8

As they approached the coordinates from the tracking device, Kevin didn't know what to expect. None of them did, actually.

At the control panel, Klyk put them on autopilot, letting them coast.

The ship drifted toward the coordinates. Behind them in the distance, another space battle flashed outside of planet Glomm. They were maybe a couple hundred thousand miles away from Glomm, but on a starship, that was right around the corner.

Once they rescued Max, they could hit the hyperdrive and be back on the alien planet in a few minutes. There was only one problem. Neither the Sfinks nor

Max was anywhere in sight.

"I don't see anything," Tara said, staring out of the viewport. Kevin glanced out as well but didn't see anything that resembled a gigantic spaceship.

Drooq came over and pointed out the spaceship window. He drew a circle in the air with his claw-hand. "Look," he said. "No stars."

Drooq was right.

In front of them, a massive sphere of black metal blotted out all the flickering specks of light behind it. It was almost camouflaged against the dark void of outer space.

"It's huge," Kevin said, his eyes widening as he took in the scope of the gigantic space vessel.

"How are we going to do this?" Warner asked.

"The Sfinks have that tractor beam," Drooq said. "Anything that gets too close gets sucked onto the ship automatically."

"We're going to sneak on board," said Drooq.

"Just like the Battle at Betelgeuse!" Phirf said, nodding his squid-head in approval. "Plus the Sfinks will be so busy with the Glomms, they'll never see us coming."

"Good thinking, boys," Klyk said. "Element of surprise. I like it!"

"Yeah, but what happens once we get inside?" Tara asked.

Drooq and Phirf both shrugged cluelessly.

"All right," she said. "Let's do this." Tara took out her freeze ray and powered it up. Kevin did the same with his freeze ray, and TJ made sure his shrink ray was charged up and ready to go.

"This is messed up," Warner said, realizing he didn't have a weapon to defend himself. "What am I supposed to use?"

"Here." Phirf tossed Warner an extra one of his photon blasters. "Don't say I never gave you anything."

Warner caught the alien ray gun and twirled it on his finger like a cowboy. "Sweet."

As they moved closer, the giant sphere lit up with a red flash, and then the tractor beam targeted their ship. The beam took over the controls, the motors slowed down to a slow whir, and all went silent as they were pulled toward the Sfinks' planet-sized mother ship.

When they got close enough, a large, square hatch slid open and their spaceship floated inside. The hatch shut with a loud, echoing clank.

"I got a bad feeling about this," Tara said, clutching the freeze ray in her hand.

"Shhhh," Drooq said. "Get ready."

Kevin could see they were docked in a large, rectangular room with twenty-foot ceilings. The room had two levels. Halfway up the walls, a metal catwalk wrapped around the loading dock. There were three doors on the ground floor, which led off into the Sfinks' enormous space ark.

Aside from Kevin and his friends, there was no
sign of life in the big room.

"Okay." Tara led the boys out into the Sfinks' loading dock. "Let's get out of here before they figure it out."

They hopped down from their spaceship and
stopped before the three doors.

"Which one do we take?" Kevin asked.

"Your guess is as good as mine," Klyk said.

"Maybe we split up," said Drooq. "Cover more
ground that way."

Tara raised her hand. "I just want to go officially on
the record to say I'm very much against that idea."

"Yeah, no splitting up," TJ said. "Don't you guys

watch scary movies?"

"Fine, we stick together," Klyk said.

Something clacked and clanged along the metal walkway up above. Kevin spun around and saw three Sfinks looking down on them from the catwalk. They raised their space pistols and aimed down at Kevin and his crew.

"What's the plan now, then?" TJ asked.

"Fight," Drooq grumbled in his deep gargling voice, as he drew out his photon saber.

"That's your plan?" Warner asked in disbelief. "We rescued you for that wisdom?"

"Lay down your weapons, humans!" one of the Sfinks yelled to them in English. The alien feline looked like an albino, with white skin and red eyes. "You are

now the property of the Sfinks!"

Kevin chuckled out loud. The Sfink's voice was somewhat hilarious, high-pitched and nasal, with a funny-sounding accent.

"Are we really throwing down our weapons for these mutant kitty cats?" Drooq asked Klyk and Phirf.

"No way," said Klyk, gripping his space pistol.

"Look out!" Kevin shouted.

NYuRP! NYuRP! The Sfinks fired their photon blasters in a flurry of high-speed light beams. *NYuRP! NYuRP!*

Kevin covered his face as the enemy fire sailed toward him and his friends.

Drooq drew out his big, hulking battle-ax with one smooth motion.

Kevin peeked between his fingers. He could barely believe what he was seeing.

The alien metal absorbed the flurry of photon blasts.

The Sfinks were about to fire again when Drooq swung his battle-ax toward the Sfinks and hurled the photon blasts back the way they came.

The beams bounced back toward the Sfinks and hit them all at the same time. The three felines flew back in a flash of white sparks, crashed into the wall, and dropped in a motionless heap.

"Whoa," Warner gasped, his jaw dropping a little. "If we do split up, Drooq's on my team." He put out his fist and Drooq gave him a fist bump.

Clink-clank-clack-clack-clank.

A dozen more Sfink soldiers scampered onto the catwalk. Phirf knelt into a crouch and fired up at the Sfinks. All three of his hands gripped a photon blaster. His squiggly arms waved in the air, shooting wildly.

PYOO-pyoo-pyoo!

Kevin aimed his freeze ray up at the Sfinks and spotted his target in the crosshairs.

NYuRP! A beam from a Sfink's ray gun headed straight for him, right in his sightline. He froze, unable to move, a deer in headlights. It was coming too fast.

PING! Klyk's arm shot in front of Kevin's face and deflected the alien fire. Klyk's forearm glowed and pulsed with some kind of force field.

Kevin wiped the sweat from his brow and gave Klyk a grateful look, retreating behind his three monstrous alien buddies. "We have to get out of here!" he shouted to his friends. He backpedaled toward the three doorways and hustled to his left. Tara, Warner, and TJ all chased after him, weaving through the Sfinks' death rays.

But as they turned the corner, Kevin saw a platoon of Sfinks appear at the end of the hallway.

"Other way!" he screamed, and everyone turned back to the loading dock. Another pack of Sfinks spilled out of the right doorway.

"Retreat!" Kevin hollered at the top of his lungs. Tara, TJ, and Warner followed Kevin through the center doorway, trailed by Klyk, Phirf, and Drooq.

They sprinted down the hallway, but another

platoon of Sfinks rounded the corner in front of them. Kevin and the gang put on the brakes and doubled back. Kevin looked behind them and saw a pack of Sfink soldiers in the doorway.

They were stuck.

A hundred ray guns were aimed at them on all sides. The Sfinks pushed in, closing the gap. "Put 'em down!" the albino Sfink shouted in his funny voice. "Put 'em down, meow!"

Kevin's heart was pounding. There was a short pause before Klyk laid down his space pistol and put up his arms.

Kevin followed, putting down his freeze ray and lifting his arms in the air.

The rest of them did the same.

The alien handcuffs hurt Kevin's wrists, cutting into his skin. A Sfink guard nudged him forward with one of its six arms, almost making him trip, while the other guard led the way. Kevin walked in a single-file line behind TJ, Tara, and Warner. All their arms were handcuffed behind their backs. The savage felines guided them down a long, straight hallway, somewhere in the lower levels of the mother ship.

"Let us go!" Warner shouted and tried to squirm out of his handcuffs. *ZAP! POW!* A sharp electric current shocked Warner's wrists and he squealed in pain.

"Don't even try it," one of the Sfinks said. "The more you fight, the harder they'll shock you."

"Where are you taking us?" Kevin demanded to know.

The other Sfink looked down at him. "Normally we send you to processing, but we have special plans for you humans."

This was no good. Kevin didn't even know where they were. They'd been taken into a number of elevators after the Sfink army separated them from Klyk, Phirf, and Drooq, who were escorted to another sector of the ship.

Klyk told them not to worry, that they would find a way to escape and rescue them, but Kevin wasn't sure if Klyk was just trying to make him feel better.

They were in a tight spot now. That was for sure, and there was no telling if they could get out of this alive. Not to mention, they still didn't have a clue where Max was being held prisoner.

As they marched along, TJ turned around to Kevin. His eyes were big and wide and worried. "What's going to happen to us, man?" he whispered to Kevin.

"I don't know, buddy," Kevin mumbled back. He

tried to think of something to say to make his friend less scared, but Kevin was pretty frightened himself.

The Sfinks escorted them through a doorway in the middle of the corridors.

"In!" one of the Sfinks ordered. The room looked like a typical cell block in a prison, except there were magenta-colored lasers crisscrossing where the bars of the jail cells would have been.

The other Sfink used a small black device that he wore around his neck to make the laser prison bars disappear for a moment. The four kids piled in one of the cells and watched as he scanned the device in front of the lock. The hot-pink laser bars appeared again. The laser wall gave off a high-voltage hum, which meant it would probably either burn or shock whoever tried to touch it.

Kevin wasn't about to find out for himself.

Except for the laser prison bars, the jail cell was a blank white box with no windows. It didn't have a bed or anywhere to sit except the floor. It didn't even have a toilet. It was utterly inhumane, but it could also mean that they weren't going to be staying here long.

One of the Sfinks left the room while the other one stayed. Kevin watched as the six-armed alien stored their confiscated weapons in a locked compartment on the wall opposite their cell.

"Hey, you big ugly thing! Let us out of here!" Tara yelled, but the Sfink just scowled at her and hissed before turning away.

Kevin pinched his eyebrows together. He had to think. But how were they supposed to escape? They were trapped like rats.

"Guys, come over here," Warner whispered. "I gotta show you something."

"What is it?" TJ asked, as they all huddled around Warner.

Warner had his hands cupped together as they gathered around.

"All right, you guys have to promise not to get mad before I show it to you."

"Why do we have to do that?"

"Just promise," Warner insisted.

"Okay, fine. We promise not to be mad!" Kevin and Tara jinxed each other.

"Me, too," TJ said excitedly. "Now show us whatcha got."

Warner opened his hands and revealed something wrapped in a black cloth. He opened the cloth, and there lay a bit of crystal about as small as a fun-size candy bar.

"Is that what I think it is?" TJ asked.

"Yup," Warner said. "How awesome is that?"

"Not awesome!" Tara punched Warner in the shoulder.

"Ouch, what was that for?"

"For being a total idiot!"

"Why am I an idiot?" Warner asked. "This thing might save our butts right now. Plus, you promised you wouldn't get mad!"

The crystal was glowing orange at the moment. Probably because they were locked in this cell, Kevin thought. He couldn't believe Warner had stolen a crystal from the cave on planet Glomm.

"Dude, what were you thinking?" Kevin asked. "We can't even see what it's trying to show us."

"We're going to tell the future with it!" Warner said.

"If you were paying attention instead of stealing sacred crystals from alien planets, then you'd know that the Glomms are the only ones who can activate the visions in the crystal," Kevin whispered angrily.

"Oh . . ." Warner looked a little crestfallen. "So all it's going to do is glow orange?"

"Or . . . ," Kevin growled angrily through clenched teeth, "it could fall into the hands of the Sfinks! Who could probably definitely figure out how to use it with all their crazy technology." He strained to keep his voice down.

"Well, I didn't know we were going to get caught by the Sfinks when I took it, did I?" Warner protested.

"Give that to me!" Kevin reached out and lunged for the crystal.

Warner pulled his hands back. "No way!"

"I'm serious, man! Give it up!" he said, grabbing at Warner's wrist.

"Who made you the boss of everyone?" Warner said, now full-on wrestling for the crystal.

"Guys, stop it!" TJ said.

"Let go!" Kevin groaned and pried up on Warner's grasp. Their hands flung apart and the crystal went flying to the front of the cell. It stopped right between two of the laser bars.

Kevin crawled across the floor and gently stretched his fingers to snag the crystal, careful not to get zapped.

He pulled the crystal back into the cell and heard the Sfink coming toward them down the walkway.

The crystal was glowing brightly in Kevin's hands.

Clip-clop-clip-clop . . . The Sfink's footsteps drew closer and closer.

"Do something, Kevin!" said Tara. "You can't let him see it!"

Kevin didn't know what to do. The crystal seemed to be glowing brighter and brighter the closer the footsteps sounded. Just before the Sfink guardsman stopped in front of their cell, Kevin did the only thing he could think of. He popped the crystal in his mouth and swallowed it down in one hard gulp.

"What's going on?" The Sfink towered over the kids, looking down at them through the red laser bars of the cell. "No funny business."

"No funny business," TJ promised for all of them.

The Sfink stared at them as he walked away from the cell.

Warner pushed Kevin's shoulder once the alien guard left them alone.

"You just swallowed the crystal!" Warner said. "Who's the dummy now?"

"Why'd you eat it, Kev?" Tara asked.

"I don't know," he said. "I just panicked."

"Don't worry about it, Kev," said TJ. "I panic all the time."

"Come on," said Tara. "We have to figure out how we're going to get out of here."

Kevin peered out through the laser prison bars at the Sfink guard by the door. There was something buzzing around outside the jail cell, and Kevin saw a plump alien insect flying around down by the exit. The Sfink caught a glimpse of the insect and cocked his head back and forth, following the alien fly like a kitten would.

"I think I might have an idea," Kevin said to his friends. He reached into his pocket and pulled out his trusty laser pointer.

He held it in his hands as though it were the key to the entire universe. He looked at his friends' faces and cracked a smile. "This is it!"

"What do you think we can do with that?" TJ asked, his eyebrows furrowed in confusion.

"This is going to get us out of here," Kevin said confidently.

"What's the plan, Kev?" Warner asked. "You think we can take out this jail cell with a little laser pointer?"

"I have to say," Tara said. "I don't think there's any way we can jam up these prison bars with that thing."

"We're not going to have to jam them up," Kevin said.

"We're going to use that Sfink's key and walk right out of here."

"And how do you propose we do that?" said Warner. "You think he's just going to hand it over?"

"These aliens are basically just big old kitty cats, right?" Kevin said, suddenly sounding like someone giving a demonstration at a science fair. "Six-armed hairless nasty-looking ones with four eyes, yes, but feline in nature nonetheless."

"Yeah, so?" TJ said.

"Well, if there's one thing I know about cats, it's that they love to chase around laser pointers," Kevin said. "I've seen it on YouTube like a million times! They go absolutely crazy for these things."

Tara gave Kevin a funny look and shook her head. She then reached out her hand and laid the back of it across Kevin's brow like a mother testing a sick child for a fever. "Are you sure you're feeling all right?"

"I've never felt better," Kevin said, a glint of hope sparkling in his eye. "Just watch and learn."

He clicked the button and aimed his laser pointer

through the pink laser bars. He waggled the tiny red dot on the opposite wall and got the Sfink prison guard's attention.

The alien feline saw the red dot jiggling on the wall and immediately dropped his weapon.

The grotesque cat went after the red dot. All four of its eyes darted side to side like a playful kitten. Kevin wiggled the dot a little faster, keeping the Sfink enticed. The red dot danced up by the ceiling, and the Sfink leaped up and pawed at the walls.

Kevin then guided the laser pointer down to the

ground quickly, and the Sfink gave chase, galloping on all eight of its limbs toward their jail cell.

The Sfink charged after the dot, its long, forked tongue hanging out of its mouth.

Kevin led the dot straight down the middle of the hall.

Just before the Sfink came streaking by their cell, Kevin led the red pinpoint straight into their cell. The Sfink followed the dot at full speed and ran head on into the laser lattice of their jail cell.

Kablammo!

The Sfink slammed into the lasers and jolted to a stop, seeming to hang in midair before dropping to the floor. The alien's body went limp and rolled to the side before lying completely still.

"Nice work, Kev!" Tara said. "Way to think out of the litter box!"

"Thanks." Kevin reached his skinny arm through the laser bars and just barely got his fingers on the device around the alien's neck.

He tried to aim the light from the device at the lock

on the jail cell, but he didn't have the proper angle.

"Come on, guys, quick, help me out!" Kevin called out.

"What do you want us to do, man?"

The gears in Kevin's head turned quickly.

"Use my eyeglasses," Kevin told them. "And TJ's, too!"

While Kevin clicked the laser key toward the lock, TJ and Tara reached their arms through the laser bars as well, each holding a pair of eyeglasses.

The beam of light from the device refracted through the lenses and hit the lock on the sensor.

Suddenly the red glowing light disappeared, and so did the lasers caging them in.

"Kevin!" TJ shouted. "You did it!"

"Nah, man." Warner patted him on the back. "We did that . . . now let's get out of here and go find Max!"

"Don't forget about Klyk and Drooq and Phirf," Tara said.

"Right," said Kevin. "But first we have to find Max. He's our top priority right now."

Warner undid the laser key device from around the neck of the unconscious Sfink and opened up the wall safe. He passed Kevin and Tara their freeze rays, gave TJ the shrink ray, and grabbed the photon blaster Phirf had lent him.

They turned toward the exit, and the spaceship's spiral door twisted open automatically. A giant Sfink loomed in the doorway. The humongous feline alien growled at them and drew his ray gun at them quickly.

ZAP!

In a flash Tara shot off a blast from the freeze ray and drilled the Sfink in the center of his chest. The six-armed beast stiffened in an aggressive, angry pose, and the four kids sprinted past the grotesque alien statue.

As they raced through the twisting labyrinth of the Sfinks' spaceship, Warner pointed at Kevin's stomach.

"Dude, look!" he said, panting to catch his breath as they ran. "You're glowing!"

Kevin stared down the front of his shirt. It glowed with the orange light of the Glomms' prophecy crystal. "Oh no!" he said. "This thing isn't going to, like, nuke my insides, is it?"

"Too early to tell," said Tara. "Until we can test for radiation poisoning . . ."

"Not making me feel better!" Kevin shouted at Tara. "Thank you very much."

"You asked." She rolled her eyes.

"I don't know about radiation," Warner said. "But

how sweet would it be if it turned you into a superhero like Spider-Man or Superman or something?"

They came to a fork in the corridor, which split off into two hallways.

"Which one?" Tara asked.

"I say left," Kevin said.

"Why do you say that?" TJ said.

"No reason," Kevin said. "It just feels right."

He started to run ahead of them, and suddenly his

 stomach stopped glowing orange and started glowing blue.

"Check it out!" TJ pointed. "Kevin's blue now!"

"Maybe it's trying to tell us where to go?" Tara suggested.

"And whatever way blue leads is where Max will be," Warner said, adding in his two cents.

"Or Klyk and Phirf and Drooq," TJ said. "Maybe it'll lead us back to them."

"We'll do whatever the crystal tells us to," Kevin said. "Come on!"

They hustled down the spaceship hallway and were soon stopped by another split in the hallway.

"Which way do we go, Kev?" Tara asked.

"I don't know," Kevin said. "Gimme a sec."

Kevin started to go right when his blue tummy switched back to orange. He tried the hallway to the left, and his stomach flipped back to blue. The four of them hightailed it down another corridor and found themselves in a new section of the mother ship.

The corridor opened up into a big engine room.

The light was dim and the spaceship was draped in shadows. There was a large pit in the center of the room. Kevin peeked down as they edged around the rim of the smooth metal pit. He saw a massive swirl of super-charged energy particles spinning at the bottom. It must have been part of the space vessel's propulsion system.

"Be careful, you guys." Kevin gestured to the propulsion pit. He wanted them out of this room immediately. If anyone accidentally fell in there, it would rip someone apart for sure.

His blue glowing innards led them to what looked like some sort of tunnel or giant drainpipe.

The four of them ducked into the dark sewer system. They had to bend down at the waist just to fit. For a while they followed the light-blue glow, but soon they passed a ladder on the wall.

After that the light-blue glow switched to orange.

Kevin backed up quickly and crouched in front of the ladder, which went into a narrow vertical pipe leading upward.

Kevin tilted his head back and looked straight up. His stomach started glowing blue once again.

They climbed up the ladder, high into the Sfinks' ship.

A little over halfway up, the crystal flashed from blue to orange and they all stopped climbing.

"Is there another way out of here except straight up?" Kevin asked, rubbing his sweaty palms against the smooth metal curves of the pipe.

"I don't think so." Warner's voice echoed through the vertical tunnel.

"Hey guys, down here," TJ called up to them. "I found something."

Kevin heard the clink of a rusted door opening. A thick wedge of bright light washed in, and they all climbed out of the pipe.

Kevin rose to his feet and stood next to Tara, TJ, and Warner. It took a second for his eyes to adjust to the light. He squinted down the passageway, which led to a wide, well-lit room with low ceilings.

The place looked like an infirmary. As they walked down the hallway, Kevin realized that was exactly what it was. It was flanked by rows of hospital rooms all the way down each side.

Inside the rooms, the bodies of wounded or injured Sfinks slept on stone slabs, connected to feeding tubes and breathing tubes and various electronic machines.

"Should we freeze ray them?" TJ asked, as they crept through the alien sick room.

"I don't think we should waste the ammo," Kevin said. "Unless one of them wakes up, obviously. . . ."

"They all seem in pretty deep sleep," Tara said. "Maybe they're all sedated. . . ."

"Maybe if you guys stop talking, we'll stand a better chance of not waking them up," said Warner, pressing his index finger to his pursed lips as they continued tiptoeing past the sleeping aliens.

At the end of the infirmary hallway, they followed Kevin's blue glowing tummy to a set of double doors.

Kevin looked through the glass window. Across the laboratory room, a slouched figure was sitting in a high-tech wheelchair.

Max Greyson, Kevin thought. He *knew* it was him.

He knew it in his gut.

Kevin's belly glowed blue as they entered through the sliding doors. The four of them strolled across the observation laboratory and stopped in front of the man in the wheelchair.

The infamous comic book writer seemed sluggish,

as though he
was heavily
sedated, like
all his energy
was being
sucked right out
of his brain.

The telepa-
thy helmet was
clamped down
over Max's head. It was
connected to a high-tech
contraption hanging down
from the ceiling.
It looked like
some kind of
computer sys-
tem connected
to a bigger
network.

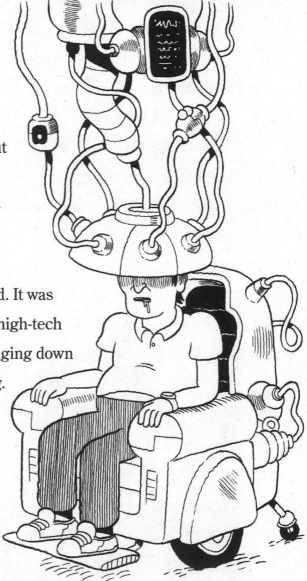

Max was hooked up here just like the Glomms had the crystal hooked up in their command center.

Kevin clutched Max by his shoulders and looked directly into his face. His eyes were all-white cue balls, rolled into the back of his head, and he was drooling down the side of his cheek.

"That's him, right?" Tara asked.

Warner examined the man's face. "Yeah, it's him," he said. "He looks in pretty rough shape, but it's him."

"How do you know?" asked TJ.

"I saw a picture of him once in *Hot Comix Monthly*," Warner responded, looking around the rest of the place.

On one side of the room, piles upon piles of sketchbooks were filled with scenes from unreleased *Brainstorm* comic books. "Jackpot!" Warner said, heading straight for the stacks of unpublished Max Greyson originals.

"We've got to get this thing off him," Kevin said. "They're sucking him dry!"

Kevin reached for the telepathy helmet, but Tara pulled him away from Max.

"Not so fast!" she said. "We don't want to short circuit him. . . ."

Tara and TJ stepped up behind the wheelchair and examined the Sfinks' contraption.

"This ain't gonna be easy," TJ said, shaking his head. "Looks complicated."

"You guys sure you can handle this?" Kevin asked.

"Are you kidding me?" Tara said. "Did you forget

who we are? We're the Extraordinary Terrestrials. . . ."

TJ shrugged at Kevin, then looked at Tara. "If you say so. . . ."

Kevin nodded and Tara and TJ went to work on detaching the telepathy helmet without frying Max's brain. Kevin walked over to Warner, who was flipping through the sketchbooks.

"Check these out, man," Warner said. "This stuff is awesome."

Kevin was about to go check out the sketches when Tara called from behind him.

"All done!" she said. "Good going, Teej!"

She high-fived TJ after he pulled the telepathy helmet off Max. Their helmet still dangled from the machine overhead.

Kevin and Warner walked over to meet the man behind the crazy future-telling comic books.

Max's eyes rolled out from the back of his head, and his face looked normal once again. He stretched his neck as the kids gathered around him. "I knew you would find me."

"Did you know we'd be in big freakin' trouble right now?" Tara asked.

"Yes," he said. "I knew that, too."

"Mr. Greyson," said Warner. "You've got to be my all-time favorite author of, like, anything ever written. . . ."

"That's nice of you to say," Max said, his voice sounding very weak before turning into a cough.

"Cool," Warner said. "I have, like, a billion questions I have to ask you."

"Sorry, guys," Kevin butted in. "No time for chit-chat. We've got to get you out of here."

"Good idea," said Tara. "This place is giving me the creeps."

"Don't forget our telepathy helmet." TJ pointed up to the high-tech headgear hanging down from the ceiling.

Tara reached up on her tippy-toes and unplugged the alien helmet. As soon as she disconnected the helmet, a security alarm activated and the room started to blink and flash with red emergency lights.

The Sfinks' alarm system rang out, blaring and

whooping throughout the ship. Kevin's stomach flashed to a bright orange.

"We have to get out of here!" TJ cried.

"Come on!" Kevin yelled, and took off down the hall with his friends close behind.

Kevin led the way, racing out of the alien hospital. TJ and Tara stayed close behind, and Max vroomed after them in his electric wheelchair. "Wait up!" Warner yelled over the blare of the alarm. His arms were full of Max's sketchbooks.

"Warner, what are you doing?"

"Do you have any clue how much I could get for these on eBay?"

"Warner!" Tara yelled at him. "Come on!"

The four kids and the comic book author skidded around the corner into another hallway that blinked with the red emergency lights.

NYuRP! NYuRP! NYuRP! Three blasts from a Sfink

ray gun streaked at them down the hall.

"Duck!" Kevin shouted, and they all hit the deck. Everyone except for Warner. As he caught up with the rest of them, the photon blasts hit the stack of Max Greyson sketchbooks he held in his arms. Warner fell back on his rear end, totally unharmed. The sketchbooks, on the other hand, were burned to a crisp, completely ruined. Warner stared at the charred remains of his precious comic book bounty and looked like he wanted to cry.

But there was no time for tears.

A pair of Sfinks appeared at the end of the hallway, firing their photon blasters again. *NYuRP! NYuRP!*

"Everybody stay down!" Tara shouted. She was next

to Kevin, lying flat on her stomach. They both had their freeze rays out, aiming them down the hallway. But they couldn't get off a clean shot.

NYuRP! NYuRP! NYuRP!

The photon blasts kept on coming. "Max, look out!" Warner shouted. The enemy fire was headed straight for the comic book author.

A quick flash of bright white lit up the hall and Max vanished. The photons hit the wall of the spaceship and singed the metal, leaving a sooty black mark.

"Nooooo!" Warner howled, thinking that Max had just been vaporized.

"Relax, Warner!" TJ said, looking up at him. He was holding the shrink ray, aiming it where Max had just been. The comic book author was now a miniature man in a tiny wheelchair.

"Max, are you okay?" Warner reached down to scoop up Max.

Max Greyson looked at Warner and gave him a thumbs-up.

ZAP! ZAP!

Kevin and Tara each fired a round of freeze-ray shots down the hall and nailed the two Sfinks, freezing them in place.

The kids scrambled to their feet and broke into a sprint, when suddenly Kevin's stomach glowed orange, and he put on the brakes. At the end of the corridor, a huge team of Sfink soldiers knocked over the freeze-rayed Sfinks.

Kevin backed away from the aliens, and his belly turned blue as they passed a door in the middle of the hallway.

"Everybody in!" Kevin called, throwing the door

open as the Sfinks started firing.

The four of them dove in, and Kevin slammed the door shut. Tara fired her freeze ray at the door and sealed them all in the room.

Kevin spun around, looking for another exit, but they were now in a storage room with no way out.

Outside the freeze-rayed door, they could hear the clippity-clop of the Sfinks' feet clattering to a stop in the hallway.

"Open!" a snarling feline voice commanded.

"No way!" TJ said, then turned to Kevin. "Why'd you lead us in here?"

"I didn't do it on purpose," said Kevin. "I just followed my gut." He pointed to his blue-glowing belly. "Literally."

"Why would the crystal lead us in here?" Warner asked. He looked down at Max Greyson in the palm of his hand. "Any thoughts, Max?"

"It has been my experience that the crystals can be very fickle," he said in a tiny, high-pitched voice. "You cannot control them or expect them to save you. They do what they must, just as we all must do."

Really? Kevin thought to himself. *That's all you got?*

"Open!" the Sfink yelled on the other side of the door. "No escape for you! Open!"

Tara turned toward the door and shouted. "Shut up, will you? We're trying to have a conversation in here!" She turned back to the boys. "Okay, seriously, what are we going to do?"

Kevin shrugged. He had no idea. His stomach was glowing blue, but he had a hard time believing that they were in the right spot.

BAM! BAM!

The Sfinks started to pound outside the door, scratching with their claws. The metallic door started to bend and dent, but then the banging stopped.

An eerie quiet filled the storage chamber, and all the kids could hear was the huff and puff of their own breath.

A few moments passed and TJ started to freak out, twitching like he was trapped in a video game glitch. He ran up to Kevin, grabbed him by his sides, and started yelling at the crystal in Kevin's stomach.

"Why are you glowing blue, you stupid crystal?" he shouted. "We're not safe in here! This is not good!"

Warner pulled TJ away from Kevin and held him by the arms. "Chill, dude, everything is okay."

"No, it's not okay, Warner, all right? This is totally not okay!" TJ yelled at him. "We're about to get caught by these Sfink things, and who knows what they're going to do to us! I just want to go home! We never should have come to outer space!"

"That's not true," Kevin said. "We didn't have a choice!"

"Yeah we did, man! We could've stayed back on

Earth and by this time I would have been at home, all snuggled up on my couch, nice and cozy, watching the science channel . . . I mean, we already saved Earth twice now. Why is it our job to save the galaxy?"

"TJ, if the Sfinks win and take over planet Glomm, then none of us are safe . . . do you get that? We're fighting for our freedom here! Our freedom to eat junk food and watch TV whenever we want!"

"I do get it, I do." TJ started to calm down. "I'm just really scared right now, that's all."

"Us, too, man," Kevin said, patting him on the back. "Us, too."

"Shhhhhhhh . . ." Tara held up her hand. "Did you hear that?"

Kevin and the boys went silent and listened closely. A noise like a buzz saw sounded beneath their feet and they all jumped back.

Sparks flew up at them as something cut out a rectangular piece from the steel floor. The kids aimed their weapons at the hole as the metal rectangle lifted up and slid across the floor.

"Freeze!" Tara yelled.

"Don't shoot!" Drooq's gruff, raspy voice hollered up from below. "It's just us!"

Relief washed over Kevin as Phirf and Klyk stuck their heads up out of the floor, too.

"How the heck did you know that we'd be here?"

"We didn't," Klyk said. "But after we broke out, and the alarm went off in this sector, we figured it must have been you guys."

"We also disabled their tractor beam," Phirf said. "In case we ever get off this ship."

KABOOM!

There was a huge explosion and the freeze-rayed

door imploded. Kevin felt himself fly off his feet. His back hit the wall and knocked the wind out of him.

The smoke cleared and the Sfinks piled in the doorway.

PYOO! PYOO! PYOO!

Klyk opened fire on the Sfinks and they jumped back into the hallway.

"Get down here!" Klyk yelled at the kids.

Kevin dropped down through the hole in the floor and counted his friends in the underground passageway. Everyone was there in one piece.

"Come on, Klyk!" Warner shouted. "We have to get back to the ship!"

"What about Max?" Klyk shouted, still firing up through the rectangular hole in the floor, keeping the Sfinks at bay. "We have to find Max or the mission's a bust!"

"We got Max already!" Warner said, holding out the miniaturized comic book genius for them to see.

Mini Max Greyson waved at them in his wheelchair. "Hello, fellas!"

"Well, why didn't you say so?" Klyk said. "Let's get out of here!"

The kids sprinted through the underground vent back to the loading dock, where their spaceship awaited their return.

Klyk fired a photon ray toward a large metal grate at the end of the tunnel, and the grate exploded out of the wall.

As they all jumped aboard the ship, the full force of the Sfinks' guard filed into the room on both levels. There were at least a hundred Sfinks.

"They're going to shoot!" Tara shrieked as the armed guard aimed at their cruiser.

Kevin leaped into action, bounding through the

cabin of the spaceship. He jumped toward the main control panel as the Sfinks opened fire. Flying in the air, Kevin extended his arm and smacked the button to activate the force field.

The ship hummed as the force field charged up.

PING! PING! ZING! ZING!

The alien gunfire pelted the force field and bounced off at crazy angles, whizzing back toward the army of Sfinks. The alien army dove for cover.

Klyk hit the engine thrusters and their spaceship propelled into hyperdrive. They shot out of the Sfinks' loading dock and back into the black void of outer space, leaving their alien nemeses in the exhaust fumes behind them.

"Quick thinking, Kevin!" TJ yelled.

Drooq and Phirf cheered and each gave him a high-five.

"Take that, you feline freaks!" Kevin pumped his fist and let out a victorious whoop.

Kevin caught his breath as he glanced back at the Sfinks' mother ship. The massive sphere rotated ninety degrees on its axis and began to move toward the battle still raging around planet Glomm.

Mini Max Greyson stood up from his miniaturized wheelchair. He struggled to keep his balance and coughed violently into his fist. Kevin went over to the comic book creator and crouched down next to him.

Tara, Warner, and TJ gathered around the man as well.

"Mr. Greyson, are you okay?" Kevin asked gently.

Max coughed again and then locked eyes with Kevin. "Please," he said, "call me Max."

"Okay, Max . . . ," Kevin said, slightly hesitant. He wasn't used to calling adults by their first names.

"Thank you all for rescuing me," Max said.

"You're welcome, Max, but first things first," TJ said, fiddling with the shrink ray's settings. "Let's get you back up to size." TJ lined up Max Greyson on the viewfinder of the shrink ray and fired the laser. The shrink ray zapped and the comic book author grew back to normal human size. "Now for your wheelchair." TJ aimed the shrink ray again, but Max stopped him.

"That's okay," he said. "I'll be all right without it."

Klyk pulled back on the accelerator for a moment so they could regroup and figure some things out. They had Max Greyson, but they needed a plan.

"Good job, everyone," said Klyk. "Now we just need to tell the Glomms that we have Max and help them fight off the Sfinks."

Just then the ship's hologram projector buzzed and crackled before the image became crystal clear. It was a Sfink, a real mean-looking ugly one, too.

"What is this?" Drooq said.

"I am Miaow, overlord and ruler of the Sfinks!" the revolting alien intoned. "You made a clever escape and rescued your precious Max Greyson, and for that I applaud you." The Sfinks' overlord made a deadpan face and slow-clapped his six hands together as if he was mocking them.

Kevin didn't like the way the Sfink was talking to them. He seemed smug—as if he knew something they didn't.

"The jig is up, Miaow! We beat you!" Tara yelled. "So cut to the chase or buzz off!"

"You will not take that tone with Miaow, little girl!" shouted the Sfink leader. "But it matters little what you say, and even less what you do."

"What's that supposed to mean?" Kevin asked. "We have Max and you don't!"

"That might have counted for something if I still needed him," Miaow cackled, and a wry smile curled up his hideous face. "I have a feeling we'll be seeing each other sometime in the *future*."

Then Miaow's image blipped out and vanished.

"What's he talking about?" Warner said.

"Don't worry about him," Kevin said. "He's just trying to get into our heads."

"Not without the telepathy helmet," TJ said, and patted the device with his hand.

"What else can you tell us about the crystals and

the Sfinks?" Tara asked Max.

"Yeah," Warner said. "And how do you know the future?"

"Are you part Glomm or something?" TJ asked.

"No, I'm not part Glomm." Max shook his head.

"Then why do you see the same future as their crystals?" Tara asked.

"Yeah," Warner said. "How'd you get like this?"

Max shuddered a little, remembering his past. "I was the unfortunate and unwilling participant of an experimental testing procedure when I was just an everyday citizen of our home planet Earth. I was a simple law enforcement officer, responding to a call about some bright lights in the sky over a local farm, when I was abducted.

"The one who abducted me . . . it was a disgusting creature. An evil creature. Some kind of insectoid. He had no emotions, no compassion, but he knew his science.

"He must have gotten his hands on some of the Glommian crystals. I do not know how. . . . He injected me with a serum made from the crystalline substance. I wasn't supposed to survive. I was just a test subject for his evil experiment, but I managed to escape. The alien came after me, tried to hunt me down. It was a nightmare. He was going to kill me, but I beat him to the punch." Max lowered his eyes to the floor and massaged his brow. "That was the first of the visions."

"All due respect, Max," Klyk spoke up. "But we don't really have time to hear your life story right now . . . unless it has something to do with the Sfinks."

"The Sfinks found me and hooked me up to some kind of supercomputer. It amplified my mind and body's new capabilities. But it wasn't a perfect system. They needed the missing piece—a telepathy helmet. As soon as they hooked me up to that, they could use my powers to mess with the crystals. I was basically a human signal to jam the frequency and accuracy of the crystals' predictions. They used me to launch their attack on planet Glomm so they could take over the cache of crystals and become the dominant force in the galaxy." Upon finishing his tale, Max took a deep breath and sighed.

"But how are they going to see the future without the Glomms?" Kevin asked.

"They have a device," Max said. "A device that mimics the light the Glomms create to see the visions."

"Okay, kids," Drooq called back from the control panel. "Story time's over . . . get your gear ready."

Kevin looked out the viewport and took in the scene. The battle for Glomm was still raging. The planet was under heavy fire from the Sfinks' battle cruisers. The Glommian fleets zipped and whizzed in the aerial firefight, defending their turf, but they were getting shot out of the sky left and right.

The Sfinks' massive spaceship hung above the planet like a giant apocalyptic moon, casting a large shadow over the surface of Glomm. Suddenly, it opened all its loading ports and launched a hundred more battle cruisers. Kevin watched with horror as the Sfinks unleashed a colossal attack.

High up in the atmosphere of planet Glomm, the fleets of alien warships clashed in supersonic battle. Photon missiles flashed and shrieked through space. Explosions of green and electric-blue plasma zapped and banged all around the planet like a laser light show's grand finale.

"Okay, listen up," Klyk said. "We have to get down to the surface. If we make it through the dogfight, we have to get to Narbok and tell him to call his troops back to the mountains to protect the crystal cave. We have to do everything we can to fight off the Sfinks."

The future of the galaxy was hanging in the balance. But one thing was for certain: Kevin and his

friends weren't going down without
a fight.

Drooq and Phirf stood by the naviga-
tion controls, preparing their flight plan.
"There's less traffic on the southwest
quadrant," Drooq said. He pointed a claw
at the radar screen.

"All hands on deck," Phirf hollered.
"We're going in!"

Drooq turned to Kevin and his friends.
"You guys ready?"

"We were born ready!" Warner said,
steely-eyed. Kevin had only seen him this
serious one other time—when he was
going for the pinball record at the arcade.

Drooq flipped on the force field again,

and the pulsating shield of energy encompassed their spaceship. Kevin felt a dull rumble as the craft charged up.

Klyk cracked his knuckles in the pilot seat.

Warner sidled up next to their cyborg friend and tapped him on the shoulder. Klyk turned around and gave Warner a puzzled look. "What?"

"Take a break, man. You owe it to yourself," Warner said. "It's my turn to fly this bad boy."

"Nice try," Klyk said. "You get to man the laser cannons."

"Aw, come on!" Warner moaned. "That's, like, kids' stuff."

"You are a kid," Klyk said.

"But I've got mad skills, though. . . ." He made a pouty puppy-dog face.

"Go." Klyk pointed to the artillery station across the ship's cabin. "Put your skills to use over there."

"Fine!" Warner said, and walked to his station.

Kevin took a seat in front of his own laser cannon. He buckled himself in and clicked on the radar monitor. Tara and TJ made sure they had their freeze ray and shrink ray ready to go. Then they sat down at their firing stations.

The engines at the back of the spaceship whooshed and shot them straight into the chaos of the battling starships. Kevin's stomach dropped. His nerves were ripe with adrenaline as he gripped the controls, keeping his thumb on the trigger button.

He glanced down at his illuminated tummy. The light from the crystal blinked from orange to blue to orange and back again.

"Here we go!" Warner shouted as their ship zoomed into the fray of swirling spacecraft.

Kevin watched a Glommian cruiser streak across

the screen in front of him, trailed by two of the Sfinks' sleek black ships. Kevin hit the button and the double-barreled laser cannons fired. The twin photon blasts narrowly missed the back of the second Sfink ship and beamed off into infinity.

"Shoot!" Kevin pounded his fist on the control panel.

"Incoming!" Phirf shouted. "Eleven o'clock!"

Their spaceship banked right and pulled up, dodging a long stream of enemy fire. *WHAM!* A loud boom rocked the cabin and Kevin jostled in his seat.

"What the heck was that?" he yelled.

"Pulsatron bomb!" Drooq shouted back. "They knocked out our force field."

"Two Sfinks heading your way, Kevin!" Tara shouted.

The enemy cruisers flew into view. He fired and nailed the back of the spacecraft with a double blast. The Sfinks' engine thrusters burst into flames, and the battle cruiser went into a tailspin.

ZHYP! ZHYP! The second Sfink cruiser returned fire and pulled up out of view. Kevin flinched as the blasts streaked toward his firing station. Klyk pulled a slick maneuver, slipping into a corkscrew so the enemy shots narrowly missed their ship.

"How d'you like that, kid?" Klyk said to Warner.

"Pretty good," Warner said. "Pretty good."

In the background of Kevin's monitor a flurry of photon beams hit a Glommian battle cruiser, ripping a gash of fire through the hull of the spaceship.

Klyk steered their ship under an attack of cannon fire, and scooted them around a friendly Glomm ship. They did a barrel roll and sped down into the atmosphere. They plunged through the stratosphere, leaving the dogfighting spaceships behind. Their ship leveled off and then headed toward the jungle, where the Glomms kept their military stronghold.

Kevin could spot the Glomms' military headquarters, above the trees, where the forest terrain ended and the craggy, otherworldly mountains housed the crystal cave.

As they descended and got closer, Kevin could see that the command center had been destroyed. Klyk

brought the ship down and hovered next to the demolished war room. *What the heck happened while they were
gone?* Kevin wondered.

Phirf hit the release button on the exit hatch and it
opened with a whoosh. Planet Glomm's gross stink filled
the cabin. Drooq jumped down first and then Klyk, both
with ray guns drawn. Phirf pushed Max and the kids
out next and then dropped down himself. Kevin's feet
hit the deck of the command center and he felt a squish.

"Blark-glark-glark-phlark," a voice said from under the soles of his sneakers.

"Huh?"

"He's telling you to get off him," TJ said.

"Who is?" Kevin looked down. He was standing in a slimy blue-green puddle. There was an exploded Glomm splattered on the floor. The alien was slowly gathering back together. There were other puddles of Glomms splattered on the floor, struggling to regenerate back to form. At least they were still alive. . . .

"Sorry . . . ," Kevin said, and backed away.

Kevin scanned the room and spotted another large puddle of Glomm on the ground. He could tell it was Narbok.

As he walked over to the Glommian general Tara and TJ peered into the main computer unit in the center of the room.

"The crystal's gone!" Tara yelled and came over to Kevin.

Kevin stopped in front of Narbok. He could see his eyes and face in the puddle of alien goop. "Are you okay, man?" Kevin asked.

Slowly a finger rose out of the ooze. "You!" Narbok bellowed and pointed at Kevin's glowing belly. "You are the chosen one!"

"No, no, no," Kevin said, lifting the alien general back to his feet. "I'm not the chosen one. I just had to swallow one of the crystals so the Sfinks wouldn't find it. . . ."

"How did you get a crystal?" Narbok's eyebrows crunched into a V.

"Warner took it from the cave!" Tara and TJ jinxed each other.

"Thanks a lot, guys. . . ." Warner stood alone and gave Narbok a sheepish grin.

"It's very bad to steal crystals from Glomm," Narbok said. "Last time someone did that, they became the most wanted criminal in the galaxy!"

He must be talking about the alien who infused Max with the crystal, Kevin thought.

"Give it back!" Narbok demanded.

"What am I supposed to do?" Kevin said.

"This is the only crystal we have. The Sfinks have taken over the crystal cave. We tried to stop them, but their forces were too much for us to handle," he said. "We need to see what the Sfinks are going to do, and we can't very well do that while it's in your stomach."

"But I don't have to go . . . you know . . . number two."

"Ew, that's disgusting!" Tara said.

"What? It's just basic biology!"

"Here." Drooq handed Kevin a bronze canister filled with liquid.

"What's this?" Kevin asked.

"It's a fizzer from the Mooymallo," Drooq told him.

"No way!" said Kevin. "I'm not drinking another one of those things!"

"It's not for your enjoyment," Klyk said. "It's to make you throw up."

"Just make sure you're in a really foul mood when you drink it," Phirf said.

That would be easy, Kevin thought. His mind was a mix of rage, panic, and pure dread. He opened the alien fizzer drink and chugged back a big sip.

It tasted so bad he almost couldn't swallow. It was as if he were licking the floor of a dirty public restroom.

"I'm going to puke!" Kevin announced as the rest of the sip dribbled out of his mouth and he heaved from the depths of his gut, vomiting profusely all over the ground. The throw-up splattered on the ground and everyone jumped back in horror and disgust.

The crystal glistened on the ground and Drooq scooped it up and wiped it off.

"Dude!" Warner said. "Gross!"

"What's the big deal?" Drooq said. "Just a little belly juice."

Kevin spat, trying to get the foul taste of the fizzer out of his mouth.

"Let me see," Narbok said.

Drooq bent down and held the crystal just above the puddle face.

Narbok attempted to view the crystal, but every ounce of energy he had was being used to restore his body back to normal.

"I can't do it," he said, giving up, exhausted.

Max said, "Maybe I can help." He took the crystal from Drooq and held it flat in his palms. Max's eyes

rolled into the back of his head and he described the vision.

"The Sfinks are everywhere. Launching attacks, taking over every planet in the galaxy, wiping out the Intragalactic Federation." Max grabbed his head. He was in a lot of pain.

"You must get inside the cave and stop the Sfinks," Narbok told them. "There's a back way through a hidden passage on the west side of the mountains."

What did they have? Kevin looked at his friends and counted their weapons. *Two freeze rays. A shrink ray. A telepathy helmet. A transmitter. Three huge aliens armed to the teeth. One Glommian spaceship. And Max Greyson.*

But seven of them against a vast army of Sfinks?

It was a tall order and easier said than done. Actually, it seemed like an impossible task, but Kevin knew there had to be a way. If science had taught him anything, it was this: if there was a way to get into a tricky situation, then there was almost definitely a way to get out of it.

"Get down!" Klyk shouted as a Sfink cruiser passed overhead.

They all ducked and hid out of sight as another Sfink cruiser buzzed past. The black ship unleashed a flurry of laser fire, and their Glomm ship exploded in a flash of fire and a burst of sparks as it fell out of the sky.

Quickly, TJ whipped out the shrink ray and aimed it up at the enemy ship. He hit the target button and the gadget zapped the flying cruiser. The shrink ray flashed and the spaceship morphed down to the size of a sofa cushion. The Sfink cruiser spun wildly and went crashing into the trees.

"**N**ice shot, Teej!" Kevin whooped and smacked his friend on the back.

TJ winced. "Thanks, Kev. But next time you want to congratulate me, can you not hit so hard?"

"Sure," Kevin chuckled. "No problem, man."

Warner gazed off to where the miniature Sfink cruiser had landed. "Let's go see if we can find it."

"Maybe we can squeeze some information out of them," Tara said, and they all walked across the bombed-out command center, leaving General Narbok behind for the time being.

There was one hover pod left intact in the rear of the war room. Klyk, Max, Drooq, and Phirf, along with

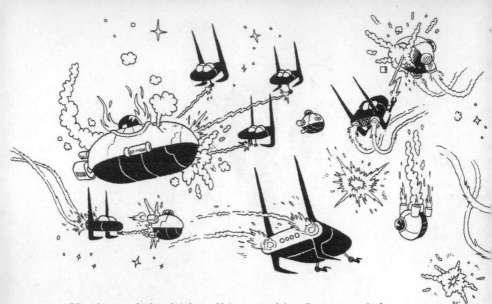

Kevin and the kids, all jumped in. It was a tight squeeze but they all managed to cram in. Drooq hit the throttle, speeding out of the rubble. He guided the hover pod down to the place where TJ had shrunk the enemy spacecraft.

Everyone hopped out of the pod and looked around. Up in space, the air battle still raged, but it looked as though the Sfinks were starting to win. *Uh-oh.*

"There's no way we're going to be able to take them all." Phirf said what everyone else was thinking. There was a long pause while everyone racked their brains for a solution.

"This is stupid; they have a device that can see the

future," Drooq said. "They're going to see us coming!"

"Well, they obviously haven't gotten it to work yet," Kevin said.

"How do you know?" Phirf asked.

"Because then why aren't they coming for us?" Kevin asked. "Like right now."

TJ shrugged. "Maybe they have bigger plans than taking out four seventh graders and a few alien bounty hunters."

"Well, I'm not waiting for them to figure it out," Kevin said. The gears were turning in his head. "What if we could use Max to jam up the crystals just like the Sfinks did?"

"It could work," TJ said. "It's basically just the same principle as EMI."

"What's EMI?" Drooq asked.

"Electromagnetic interference," said Tara. "It's like when a radio signal disturbs your TV, or your cell phone."

"You can intentionally jam a signal if you have the right equipment," said Warner.

"That's basically what they were doing with Max," Kevin agreed. "With his powers and the telepathy helmet hooked up to some kind of transmitter, they were able to jam the crystals' future-telling powers in the cave while they beat the Glomms."

"We'll have to rig up the helmet somehow so Max can transmit his own signal," Tara said.

"You think you can do that?" Klyk asked skeptically.

"We have a transmitter," Warner said, producing the alien device they'd found at Max's house the day before back on Earth. "If it can send us a comic book from outer space, then why can't it transmit Max's psychic brainwaves, too?"

"Even if we could, Max couldn't handle that right now," TJ said. "He's in pretty rough shape. Do you think he's up for it? Look at 'im!"

TJ was right. After his captivity with the Sfinks, Max wasn't looking so good.

"He'll be fine." Klyk patted Max on the back. "Won't you, old boy?"

"If this is the only way," said Max, "then I will do what I must."

"You guys, I really think this could work!" Kevin said enthusiastically.

"So what?" Drooq said. "That's not a plan. Who cares if they can't see the future if we don't have any backup?"

"Drooq's right," said Phirf. "We're going to need assistance no matter what happens."

"What about the Sfinks' communication blocker?" Kevin asked. "What if we blew that up? We could disable their communications and call the IF."

"How are we supposed to do all that?" TJ asked.

"We could fly," Kevin said, a sparkle in his eye.

"You can't fly one of our craft through those corri-dors," Phirf said. "It's way too big. That's silly."

"Not if we use the miniature Sfink fighter craft that TJ shot down," Tara said.

"I'll totally fly that thing!" Warner shouted.

"Great," said Kevin. "Let's go get it. Tara and TJ, you guys get started on the telepathy helmet and transmitter."

"I can draw you a map," said Max. "So you can find their communications center."

"We'll watch the perimeter," Klyk said, nodding to his partners. "Look out for the Sfinks."

Without a second to spare, Tara sat down on the ground with the telepathy helmet in her lap. TJ held out the transmitter and handed it to her.

"It looks like if we connect these two wires to the two conductors on the transmitter, then maybe it'll let us . . . ," TJ said.

"Gimme the tool kit, Teej," said Tara. "And let me do my thing."

TJ quickly reached into the vintage fanny pack on

his hip and handed Tara a small case that contained a small screwdriver, some copper wire, a few tiny screws, and a miniature pair of pliers. Tara picked up the pliers and went to work tinkering with the alien technology.

"Hey Kevin, do you still have that laser pointer?" Tara asked.

"Yep." Kevin patted his pockets, pulled it out, and handed it over.

She leaned over the two devices, holding her mini pliers, and linking them together with parts from the laser pointer. She bit her tongue as she pried at one of the silvery metallic panels on the side of the helmet. She looked a bit insane, her tongue drooping out of the side of her mouth, her face scrunched and contorted, with one eye bulging out of its socket. She always looked like this when she was trying to solve a complicated problem.

"All right, Kev," said Warner, waving him over. "Let's go find that Sfink battle cruiser that TJ shot down."

Kevin followed Warner into the jungle.

It didn't take long to find the cruiser crashed in the dirt. Warner ran over to the mini ship. They crouched down as two Sfink pilots hopped out, bewildered and confused at what had just happened. Warner lined up his index finger with one of the Sfinks and flicked the tiny alien into a patch of thick grass. He flicked the other one in the opposite direction.

"See ya," he said. "Wouldn't want to be ya!"

The boys returned to the group with the shrunken cruiser, and Tara was almost finished. The transmitter was secured to the top of the telepathy helmet.

Tara glanced up after another minute. "Here we go."

"Hope this works." Kevin crossed his fingers.

"But wait—his brain could short out," Warner said. "And he needs his brain to make comics . . . for me."

"Quit being selfish, Warner," Kevin said. "This isn't about comics; this is about saving the galaxy."

Max turned to Warner. "It's a risk I'm willing to

take if it means saving us, saving everyone from those awful things."

Tara walked over and placed the helmet on Max's head. She flicked the switch and the helmet buzzed to life. Max focused his energy on the crystal, which Drooq held. The stone started to flicker, zapping back and forth from orange to blue.

"Okay, good," Kevin directed the comic book author. "Now just start backing up."

Max backed away from the crystal, and when he reached about ten yards away, the crystal stopped flickering and returned to its orangey glow.

"He's only effective in close proximity," TJ said. "That's why we have to get him inside the cave. That'll be up to you guys." He pointed to Klyk, Phirf, and Drooq.

"So all we have to do is fly back into the Sfink mothership and blast the computer that controls their communications system?" said TJ.

"Yup." Kevin raced over to the miniaturized space-ship. "Who's coming with me?"

"Well, we know I'm flying," Warner said, and ran over to stand next to Kevin.

"I'm in," Tara said.

"Me too," said TJ.

"Here," Max said, giving them a detailed map of their route inside the Sfinks' mother ship. "Take this and follow the path into sector seven." The comic book author took a step back and saluted them. "Good luck."

"Good luck to you, too, Max," Kevin said.

TJ handed the shrink ray to Klyk and stood next to his friends.

Kevin, Warner, Tara, and TJ all held hands and closed their eyes while Klyk lined them up in the view-finder of the shrink ray. "My, how things come full circle sometimes." Klyk cracked a smile and zapped the kids down.

Kevin opened his eyes and looked up at Klyk, Phirf, and Drooq. They looked like hundred-foot-tall giants looming over them.

"Good luck," Klyk said. "You're going to need it."

"We all are," Kevin said and then turned and boarded the black battle cruiser with his three friends.

Kevin sat next to Warner in the copilot seat. TJ and Tara were crammed in the backseat. TJ nudged her. "Scoot over," he said. "You're taking up too much space."

"Ready, Warner?" Kevin asked and took a deep breath.

"All systems check," Warner said. "We got the invisibility shield activated. This is going to be a stealth mission, guys. In and out as quick as we can." He scanned the map Max had drawn for them. "We're going to cruise into sector seven and take out their communication interceptor."

Warner hit the
controls, and the
cruiser leaped off
the ground and soared into the air.
It was a little wobbly at first,
but he quickly got the
hang of it.

The flight
smoothed out and
Kevin looked down below.

Klyk, Phirf, and Drooq were standing with Max at
the base of the mountain range. Kevin watched from
way up as the three aliens and the comic book author
entered the side of the mountain through a small cavern.

Down below they could see a giant bluish-green
puddle of Glomm soldiers splattered on the ground
around the mountain, squiggling and squirming, trying
to regenerate.

This better work, Kevin thought as they zoomed invisibly up toward the giant black sphere. *Or else we are all going to be in big trouble.*

"See that open air dock on the bottom hemisphere?" Tara gave instructions. "Take that!"

"Got it!" Warner cruised inside the Sfinks' mother ship undetected.

They flew through the port and into the depths of the outer shell.

"Take the next right," Tara said.

Warner banked their invisible cruiser right at the

end of the spaceship's corridor. "Whoa," he said, and pulled back on the throttle, slowing down as two Sfinks marched at them down the hallway.

Warner swerved around the giant Sfink's legs and then lifted the ship up as high as it could go without hitting the ceiling.

"Left!" Tara shouted out. "Now!"

Warner swiveled the controls with his left hand and they zipped around the corner.

"Okay," Tara said, "now take the next left, and the control center should be about halfway down the hallway."

They propelled around another corner and stopped in front of the door to the control room. They hovered in midair, looking through the window. Three Sfinks manned three different control panels inside the room.

Kevin gulped. *How were they supposed to get inside the room?* They hadn't thought of that. His only comfort was the fact that he knew they were protected by the invisibility shield.

"Bingo!" Warner said, as one of the Sfinks rose out

of his seat and made his way to the door.

The Sfink walked out and Warner dipped down and glided in between the closing double doors.

While the two other Sfinks stared at their computer screens, monitoring the communications system, Warner guided the cruiser to the main computer module and hovered over it for a moment.

"Engage target," Kevin said.

Warner tapped the control panel, and the laser cannons lined up at the back of the Sfinks' computer system.

"Ready," Kevin said.

"Aim," said TJ.

"Fire!" Tara said.

Warner launched the photon missiles at the back of the computer. The machine erupted into flames and blew the two Sfinks out of their chairs. The kids' mini cruiser soared backward from the explosion, too.

Warner spun them around toward the door and they whizzed toward it. Just then, the third Sfink ran back into the room to see what was wrong, and they zoomed past him and back into the hallway of sector seven.

"Whooo!" Kevin shouted as they cruised down the corridor back the way they came.

"Way to go, guys!" Tara high-fived TJ in the backseat.

"We did it!" TJ shouted.

"Next left!" Tara navigated them back toward the docking port.

They sailed around the corner.

WHAM!

The face of an enormous Sfink came into the view and they nailed it at full speed. The humongous alien howled and whapped one of its six arms at the invisible craft.

Their battle cruiser careened into the wall and clattered to the floor. Kevin felt a surge of energy fail around their ship as the invisibility shield shut off. *This isn't good*, Kevin thought. His stomach dropped as he remembered he was the size of a mouse with a giant alien cat lurching after them.

Now exposed, Warner hit the thrusters and lifted off the ground as the Sfink pulled out his space pistol

and started shooting at them.

They flew down the hallway, the Sfink sprinting behind them, firing photon blast after photon blast, trying to take them down.

NYuRP! NYuRP! NYuRP!

Warner dodged and weaved through the blasts whizzing by the ship.

"Right!" Tara shouted, and they made a hard right, almost crashing into the far wall.

They shot into the loading dock and Warner accelerated through the open hatch and back out into the atmosphere of planet Glomm.

"**P**hew!" Kevin wiped the sweat from his forehead as they descended toward the cave of crystals. Their cruiser accelerated faster and faster, speeding away from the Sfinks' mother ship.

"Hold on to your hats," Warner hollered.

"We're not wearing hats," TJ said.

"It's just an expression," said Tara.

"Duh, I knew that," said TJ. "I was just messing with him. . . ."

"Come on, TJ," Kevin said. "Get your head in the game."

"Okay, coach!" TJ quipped.

Kevin raised his eyebrow, not amused. "Guys, focus.

And be on the lookout for Sfinks."

Putting the ship into a lower gear, they flew into the back passage of the crystal cave. Their cruiser was silent. Their lights were off, and the cave was pitch-dark, making it hard to see anything that might be coming up ahead.

They slowed at the end of the narrow opening, where the light from the glowing crystals shone through. The light flickered back and forth between orange and blue. Max's interference must be working.

Idling in midair, Warner turned the nose of the battle cruiser around the corner and saw two Sfinks marching along the dimly lit tunnel.

They swerved through the small tunnel opening to the main cave, undetected by the roaming Sfinks. They hovered near the high ceiling. Down below Kevin could see the Sfinks' leader, Miaow, approach his newfound fortune. Two Sfinks knelt down and placed a device in front of the pulsing blue-orange crystals. It was clear that they were trying to fix the device so they could see into the future, but the crystals were on the fritz. Miaow yelled at them in some high-pitched alien language.

If only Miaow knew, Kevin chuckled to himself.

"I think I see our friends," Tara said. "Warner, seven o'clock."

In the back of the cave, Klyk, Phirf, and Drooq were hiding behind an outcropping of crystal stalagmites. They were circled around Max, who had on the telepathy helmet. The man looked like he was in a trance as he transmitted the signal. Warner swooped down to join them.

Kevin opened the hatch of the cruiser as they hovered at eye level with their alien friends. "Is he okay?"

"I don't know, but I think it's working," Drooq replied.

"How'd it go out there?" Klyk asked.

"The communication blocker is done-zo," Warner said.

"Now that the satellites are disabled," Klyk said, "the IF should be on their way."

"How do you know that?" Kevin asked.

"Whatever messages they intercepted would now finally get to their original destination," Phirf said. "The IF is probably getting flooded with requests."

Phirf turned on his interstellar radio and dialed a number. "There's a busy signal."

"Try to call someone else to see if it's working," Kevin said.

Phirf dialed another number.

"Who are you calling?" Warner asked.

"Just my wife . . . ," said Phirf.

Tara made a funny face. "You have a wife?"

Phirf put a finger to his mouth and shushed them. "Hey darling, just calling to see if the line's working. Having some reception problems . . . Oh, you know, everything's fine. In a little tangle with some Sfinks, but nothing to worry about. IF's almost here. Yeah, yep . . . uh-huh . . . got it! Love you, too, baby!"

They were all staring bug-eyed at the alien as he hung up the call.

"What?" Phirf shrugged.

Just then a deafening air-raid siren blared, echoing throughout the cave.

"What's the meaning of this? I want to know what's going on meow, right meow!" Miaow threw his paws into the air, sending all his troops out of the cave to see what was wrong.

But Kevin knew the IF was already here.

As the Sfinks rushed outside, Warner steered their miniature cruiser after them, hovering at the mouth of the cave. There were IF spacecraft everywhere, filling up the sky. The federation forces had been dropped to the surface of the planet, and headed toward the crystal cave.

The Sfinks weren't backing down. The six-armed feline aliens charged, clashing with the IF troopers in a dazzling blaze of laser rays.

The sky flashed with light as IF warships and the Sfinks' battle cruisers blasted away at each other with their photon cannons.

Kevin glanced down and saw three Sfinks setting up what looked like some kind of high-tech rocket launcher.

"Over there!" Kevin shouted. "Shoot their rockets!"

The Sfinks were aiming at a group of IF troops near the mountain range. Warner rotated their ship in the air, and TJ fired the cannons. The mini laser blasts sailed down and drilled the Sfinks' weaponry. The alien rockets exploded and the Sfinks went flying, flailing through the air, their rocket launcher destroyed.

"Yeah!" Kevin shouted. "Direct hit!"

"You guys, let's go back inside!" Tara said. "It's too dangerous out here. Don't forget we're still little!"

"Are you kidding?" Warner said. "This is awesome!"

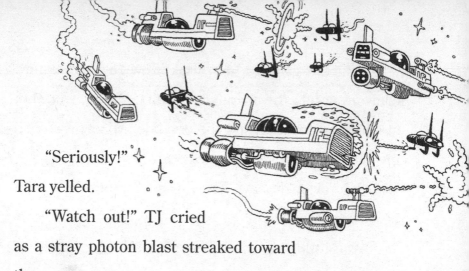

"Seriously!"
Tara yelled.

"Watch out!" TJ cried
as a stray photon blast streaked toward
them.

Warner jerked the controls and they jolted out of
the way as the laser beams scorched the mountainside.

"Okay, that was a close one." He whirled the ship
around and flew back into the cave.

Miaow was the only Sfink left inside. It was time
to close in on the most
repulsive

villain in the galaxy. As Warner flew their miniature cruiser out into the open, Klyk, Phirf, Drooq, and Max stepped out from behind the crystals. Miaow was furious, nearly spitting with rage.

"It's over, Miaow," Kevin said from the mini spaceship.

"You little mouserats!" The Sfink leader turned to look up at the tiny ship. "What have you done?"

"It's kind of self-explanatory," Warner said. "Isn't it?"

"This wasn't how it was supposed to be," Miaow said, letting out a hiss and a snarl.

"Yeah, well, the future's not always what it's cracked up to be," Warner said.

"What do you know about the future, tiny little idiot boy?" Miaow said.

"More than you, apparently," Kevin said.

"Well, I knew a little bit myself," Miaow said coyly.

"Knew?"

"Obviously you didn't know enough," Kevin said.

"It's not about what I knew," said Miaow. "It's about what you'll soon find out."

"I'm getting a little sick of this guy's attitude," Drooq said, and trained a freeze ray on the Sfink overlord.

"Can you please stop pointing that at me?" Miaow said. "You're making me itchy."

"What's the matter, Miaow?" Drooq said. "Got fleas?"

"I never!" Miaow sounded offended. "But it's just that when I get itchy I get twitchy and when I get twitchy there's no telling what I might do. . . ."

Miaow held up something in his hand.

"What's that?"

"What this?" Miaow said. "It's just a little mechanism that—should I press this button right here—will blow this whole place to bits, crystals and all."

"You went through all this trouble just to blow it all up?"

"No, you imbecile, this is my failsafe in case anything went wrong," Miaow said. "I wanted the crystals so I could take over the galaxy, but somehow you stopped me from doing that. Well, if that's how you want to play it, fine, but if I don't get the crystals, then no one does."

"That's crazy!" TJ yelled. "Those crystals share the same life force as the Glomms. If you destroy the crystals, the Glomms get wiped out, too!"

"Really?" Miaow smiled. "Then I guess that's just an added bonus. Never liked those stinking sacs of ooze."

"I'm about to ice this guy," Drooq said.

"That would be unwise," said Miaow. "A Sfink's reflexes are ten times faster than any of yours are. By the time you freeze me, you'd all be blown to bits."

"Take it easy now, Miaow." Kevin said. "Let's just talk this thing through."

Just then the IF ground troops stormed the mouth of the cave. Their ray guns were drawn. Kevin heard a voice call out in the Sfinks' native language, a high-pitched, fast-paced string of irritating sounds, coming from a loudspeaker outside.

"What are they saying?" Kevin asked Klyk from the cockpit of the cruiser.

Klyk flipped his language chip to Sfink and listened, repeating, "We have the place surrounded. Put down your weapons. Come out of the cave with your hands up. You are under arrest."

"Stop!" Klyk shouted at them. "He's got a bomb!"

The alien SWAT team paused on the threshold of the cave.

"Miaow, if you set that bomb off, you're going to die, too," Kevin pleaded.

"I'm pretty sure I'll survive," said Miaow.

"Oh yeah, how's that?" TJ said. "What makes you invincible?"

"Oh, I don't know," said Miaow. "Maybe the fact that I'm not even here."

"What are you talking about? You're standing right in front of us," Kevin said.

"No, I'm not," he said. "I'm back on the ship."

"I told you he was crazy," Tara said.

"Crazy enough to design an android that looked exactly like me? Send him out to do my dirty work, so I never get hurt? You can call it crazy, but I prefer to call it genius."

The Miaow in front of them then pressed a button on his cheekbone to reveal the computerized circuitry behind his face, running through his whole body. The Sfink in front of them wasn't really a Sfink at all. It was only a robot Sfink. It didn't matter if it got blown to bits!

"I'll tell you what," Miaow said. "You have impressed me. So I'm feeling playful and in a fun mood. What would really impress me is if you and your gang can get out of the cave before it goes boom."

"He's gonna do it!" Klyk screamed up at the kids' mini cruiser. "Get outta here!" Drooq and Phirf sprang into action, pulling on Max and running out of the cave.

Warner hit the accelerator and spun them around in the air. The engines thrust them full-throttle toward the crowd of IF soldiers. The IF team ran toward the opening of the cave.

As they flew out, the bomb detonated and the blast

shook
the
ship.
Warner
lost con-
trol in the
huge puff of
dirt and rocks, and
they slammed hard into
the rubble. Below them, Klyk, Phirf,
Drooq, and Max went flying wildly into the air from the
blast.

The kids waited in suspense, buried in the alien rubble.
What if the shrink ray had been destroyed, or there
was no one left to make them normal size again? It was
completely dark underneath the dirt—what if they were
stuck here?

"Is everyone okay?" Kevin asked in the pitch black.

"I think so," Warner said.

"I'm good," TJ said.

"Me, too," said Tara.

A few seconds later, their battle cruiser shifted and lifted up. Daylight shone through the windshield of the cockpit. The nose of their ship was pointed straight down at the ground, and Kevin had to hold on tight as everything shook.

A disgusting alien face stared at them through the viewport.

"Drooq!" Kevin and his friends cheered as their alien buddy set them on the ground. Kevin opened the side door of the cockpit and looked up at Klyk, Drooq, Phirf, and Max, who was alive but appeared to be in his own world. "What happened to the crystals?"

"Gone, I'm afraid." Phirf hung his head, and Klyk cast his eyes down at the ground.

"What about the Glomms?" Tara asked from the back of the cruiser.

The three aliens shrugged, a bit shell-shocked and covered in dirt.

"We have to go check. Warner, take us up to the command center," Kevin said, closing the hatch as his friend started the engines.

They rose up off the ground and flew to the bombed-out command center. Their tiny ship cruised over to the spot where General Narbok had been.

There seemed to be no life in the gelatinous glob that was once the head of the Glomms. Kevin heard a sniffle from the backseat. He turned around and Tara and TJ were both starting to cry.

Kevin's eyes welled up a bit as he stared down at the puddles of Glomms splattered across the floor.

"Good-bye, Narbok," Kevin said and wiped the tears from his eyes.

On the floor below, Narbok's eyeballs opened up

and his mouth took shape in the gathering puddle.

"I'm not going anywhere," the Glommian general said to the ship floating above him.

"Narbok! How are you alive?" Warner said. "The Sfinks destroyed the crystals. . . ."

Narbok gasped. "They did?"

"No, they didn't," TJ said. "Look!"

They all peered out of the command center, down to the demolished mountain range. Through the cracks and crevices of the rubble, a faint blue glow shone up at the sky.

"How is that possible?" Warner asked. "Miaow bombed the place sky-high!"

"And yet the crystals remain," Narbok said. He was slowly starting to gain his form back on the ground.

"The core must be indestructible," Warner said.

"Or stronger than we thought," said Tara.

"Or maybe the future just can't be destroyed," TJ said loftily.

Kevin didn't know how the crystals had survived, and for the first time in his life, when it came to something scientific, he didn't really care. Sure, he wanted to know the answer, but he could wait to find out.

You don't have to know everything all at once, he thought. And it dawned on him that being a know-it-all could be a very dangerous business.

A new sort of wisdom took him over as one of the Intragalactic Federation starships descended over the wrecked command center. Klyk, Drooq, Phirf, and Max walked down the high-tech hover steps and onto the platform.

Warner lowered their mini cruiser to the floor, and the tiny science campers jumped out. From behind the group, a fourth alien walked down to greet them. "Kevin, Warner, Tara, TJ," Klyk said. "I'd like to introduce you to the commanding officer of the Intragalactic Federation, Byzi."

"Hello, sir." Kevin nodded respectfully.

"Hi," said TJ.

"Howdy," said Tara.

"Yo," Warner said. "Whatup, man?"

Byzi looked like the type of alien you might see in

a Hollywood movie: short, gray, wrinkled skin, spindly arms and legs, wide head with big black saucer eyes.

The head of the IF gestured to Klyk.

"Oh yeah, before we forget." Klyk pulled out the unshrink ray and aimed it at Kevin and the gang. He fiddled with the controls. "Uh-oh . . ."

"What's that mean?" TJ asked.

"I think it's broken," Klyk said. "Looks like you guys are going to be itty bitty until we find another one."

"Are you kidding me?" Warner asked. "I'm gonna be the smallest kid in school!"

"I'm just messing with you," Klyk said. "It works."

"Check it out, guys!" Tara said. "Klyk made a joke!"

"Hahaha," said TJ.

"So funny I forgot to laugh."

Klyk aimed the alien device at the kids and zapped them back to full size.

"What brave humans here stand before me," Byzi said. "Thanks to your efforts, the galaxy is a safe place once again."

Byzi cleared his throat and continued.

"We now have the Sfinks under control, and we're going to make sure they never get out of hand again," the head of the IF went on.

From atop the bombed-out command center, Kevin looked down on the scene below. The Glomms were beginning to rise from their puddles and take shape once again. The IF forces were rounding up the Sfinks and throwing them into spaceships to take them to space prison, where they belonged.

Kevin looked up, and the sky was calm and free from the Sfinks' warships. The federation starships hovered in the atmosphere, some of them docking on the Sfinks' mother ship to raid the remaining Sfinks. Most of the Sfinks were already on the ground under arrest.

The nasty feline aliens each had six arms shackled behind their back, hissing and snarling at the alien police officers barking orders at them.

"Hopefully we don't run out of handcuffs." Byzi chuckled.

"Good one, sir." Klyk laughed a little aggressively.

Byzi ignored him and looked up at the kids.

"I commend you for your excellence in the heat of battle and hereby make you honorary members of the Intragalactic Federation." He produced four pins in his long spindly hand, and Kevin and his friends accepted them.

Warner looked at his IF pin, turned it in his hands, and made a face. "That's all we get? A lousy pin?"

Kevin elbowed his friend, while trying to keep a smile on his face. "This is the head of the IF, dude. Just take the pin and say thanks."

"What else can we give you?" Byzi said. "Anything at all?"

Kevin looked at his friends, and they all nodded at one another.

"We want to go home," Kevin said. "Back to Earth."

"Wait," said Warner. "Was that what you guys were thinking? 'Cause I totally thought we were trying to get our own spaceship."

"We can't give you a spaceship," Byzi said.

"Aww, man!" Warner groaned.

"Your planet doesn't belong to the Intragalactic Federation," he said. "Your leaders would rather lie about the existence of others in the galaxy outside their own people. Absolutely ridiculous. You are the first humans to ever be members of the IF. Just don't tell your leaders. I hear they can be pretty cruel to people who believe in aliens."

"But how are we going to get home without a space-ship?" TJ asked.

"We got you covered," Klyk said, and Phirf and Drooq both nodded.

"These boys will take you home in a brand new spacecraft. But right now I have to get back to work. There is a lot of cleanup to be done. And don't even get me started on the paperwork."

Byzi marched back up into his starship and turned to face them. "Farewell, young humans, and thank you again for your service to the galaxy."

The starship doors closed, and Byzi flew away back to the surface.

A few minutes later, a brand new, gleaming space cruiser arrived to take them home.

"Sweet!" Warner said.

"What do you say, guys?" Klyk said. "I think we should let Warner fly home."

"Really?" Warner's eyes lit up.

"Nah!" Phirf and Drooq both laughed, weird alien

cackles, but laughter nonetheless.

"I'm starting to like these guys," Tara said.

"Ready to go?" Kevin asked, turning to his friends.

"Yeah," said Tara. "We totally are."

Kevin walked up to Narbok, who was half formed on the floor, along with the other Glomms, who were slowly but surely putting themselves back together.

"I don't know how we did it, but we did it," Kevin said.

"Because of you, Kevin," Narbok said. "You believed we could win, and so we did."

"It was a little more than that," he said. "We all had a lot to do with it."

Kevin reached down to Narbok and shook his hand,

which was growing out of a blob on the floor. He then knelt down and gave him a hug. His face squished into the side of the Glomm general's goopy skin. He let go, and Tara tried to give Narbok a hug, too, but Kevin stopped her.

"Not a good idea," he whispered. "Kinda nasty, actually."

"Well, so long!" She waved good-bye instead.

They turned away from the alien general and walked onto their new spaceship.

Kevin wished he had one of those fizzer drinks to try again. He bet it would taste pretty good right about now.

The spaceship door closed behind him, and Kevin sat down next to his friends and Max while Klyk, Phirf, and Drooq started the engine.

The spaceship then lifted off the ground and soared up into the sky, away from the distant alien planet, and into the wormhole superhighway that would take them home.

The spacecraft entered Earth's atmosphere in the middle of the night. They had been gone for what felt like a day at the most, but Kevin soon realized it had been a few more than that.

When Klyk lowered them down over their science camp, Kevin and his friends looked down and saw the whole area lit up with floodlights. There were police cars and search parties all over the place.

"Holy cow," TJ said. "Are they looking for us?"

"I don't know, man," Kevin said.

"Klyk, can we get some surveillance down below?"

Klyk hit a few buttons and zoomed in on the scene beneath them. There were police questioning all the counselors. Mr. Dimpus, the camp director, was surrounded by cops in blue uniforms. Alexander, the nerd bully, was in a straitjacket, and was getting lifted into an ambulance. All the other campers and their parents were off in search parties.

"Looks like we're going to have some explaining to do," Tara said.

"Or," Klyk said, "you could just say you got lost in the woods."

"Are you kidding me?" Warner said. "How are we not going to tell everyone that we saved the universe?"

"Because you might end up like that kid down there going to the loony bin," Max said.

"Good point," said TJ.

"I'll drop you off away from everybody, and you can walk back," Klyk said. "Sound good?"

"I can't believe this is it," Kevin said. "Klyk, Drooq, Phirf. I'm gonna miss you guys."

"Awww," Tara said. "This is sad."

"I know, right?" TJ said, wiping a tear from his eye. "I hate good-byes."

"We'll miss you guys, too," they said.

"And Max," said Warner. "Do you think we're ever going to get another comic book about us?"

Max laughed. "Eventually," he said. "But probably not as fast . . . don't worry about me. Go back to your families; I'm sure they're worried sick."

"Right," said Kevin.

Klyk guided the spacecraft down to the earth's surface, away from the hectic bustle of the search parties. The kids hopped down into the dirt of their home planet.

Kevin glanced back for one last look at the spaceship as it soared off, zipping away into the sky. The four kids walked through the woods until they came upon the search party headquarters at the center of camp.

They paused at the edge of the forest, taking it all in. Soon they would be back with their friends and reunited with their parents. There would be a million and one questions they would have to answer. Right now, they had no idea how they were going to answer them—but they were scientific geniuses and heroes of the galaxy—they would figure it out.

ACKNOWLEDGMENTS

Special thanks to Hayley Wagreich, Josh Bank, and Sara Shandler for helping me figure out the future of the galaxy; to Alice Jerman and Emilia Rhodes for pushing me past the limits of the solar system; and to Ryan Harbage for his zen-like understanding of the cosmos. You have all helped save the known universe from complete and utter destruction, and for that we are all grateful.